Love and Kisses
Christmas
Collection

Christmas Wedding Wishes
Second Chance Christmas
Mistletoe Kisses

Three heartwarming, sweet, romantic tales of love that will warm your heart on a cold winter night. You will truly believe Christmas is a time for dreams to come true and for miracles to happen!

Other Titles by Debra Elizabeth

Love & Kisses
Christmas
Collection

3
COMPLETE
STORIES

Christmas Wedding Wishes

~~~

Second Chance Christmas

~~~

Mistletoe Kisses

DEBRA ELIZABETH

LOVE AND KISSES
CHRISTMAS COLLECTION

ISBN-13: 978-1981665174
ISBN-10: 198166517X

Cover Art Designs, Interior Layout and Formatting by Terry Roy

Contents

After being left at the altar, Callie Spencer needed a fresh start. She accepted a position as the Children's Librarian in a small Vermont town.

Single dad Tom Sullivan was too busy raising his 4-year-old daughter to look for love, but all that changed when he meets Callie. Can these two fragile souls find love and heal their broken hearts?

Megan Duffy needed to get away after a broken engagement and a few days at her family's cabin could be just what she needed. She was looking forward to the peace and quiet, that is, until she meets hunky storeowner Ryker McCabe.

Can Ryker put the light back in her eyes and heal her broken heart?

Ellie Davison had the worst luck when it came to dating. Not wanting to endure any more bad first dates, she swore off dating, that is, until she met the impossibly handsome Jared at her friend's wedding.

Corporate lawyer Jared Castian was not pleased when his Washington firm transferred him to Boston to oversee a complicated merger. He was on the fast-track to making partner and had no time to date. When a chance meeting at his friend's wedding paired him with bridesmaid Ellie Davison, he found himself captivated by the pretty brunette. Was Ellie the one that would open his heart to love?

Acknowledgements

A SPECIAL THANKS GOES TO MY dearest friend, Sandy Hart, who has patiently read every romance story I've written even though romance is not particularly her favorite genre. Your encouragement and comments have made the book infinitely better.

And lastly, many thanks go to my wonderfully talented graphic artist, Terry Roy. She is a wizard when it comes to book covers and paperback editions.

DEBRA ELIZABETH

CHRISTMAS
Wedding
WISHES

A NEW ENGLAND ROMANCE

Chapter 1

CALLIE MARIE SPENCER INHALED DEEPLY as she finished dressing in the bridal room. A gentle breeze wafted into the room. "I love the smell of spring. Couldn't have asked for a more perfect April day."

She couldn't keep the smile from her face as she looked in the mirror while Anna adjusted the veil over the golden brown curls brushing her shoulders. Her strapless a-line silk gown adorned with crystal and pearl beading along the hem was gorgeous in its simplicity. She had known the minute she saw it hanging in the bridal salon that this was the wedding gown she wanted. Everything about it was perfection. Adding the fingertip veil with matching crystals along the border was the final touch to her ensemble. The crystals would sparkle in the light as Callie walked down the aisle on the arm of her beloved brother, Shawn, to marry the man of her dreams. She was beyond happy.

"You look so beautiful," Anna said, securing the veil with a few pins.

"Thank you, Anna."

Anna Brown had been her best friend since the second grade, when her family had moved into the house across the street in their small Connecticut town. They had shared everything through the years from schoolyard games to girl scouts to first crushes. They confided in each other about everything. Callie couldn't imagine anyone else filling the shoes of maid of honor on her special day.

She glanced at Anna, who looked beautiful in her floor-length lavender chiffon dress. The color was stunning and complemented her dark hair and porcelain skin to perfection.

"Wait until Ethan sees you," Anna said.

"Mrs. Callie Donovan has such a nice ring to it, don't you think?"

"Absolutely."

Callie hugged her dearest friend. "Thank you for everything. I couldn't have done all this without you."

"You can stop thanking me now. You know I wouldn't be anywhere else. It's been so much fun planning your wedding and just look at you. You're a vision. I've never seen a more beautiful bride."

The girls' tender moment was interrupted when Callie's phone pinged.

"I bet that's Ethan sending me a heart text," Callie said as she walked to the table to retrieve the phone. "He's always sending them to me. I love that he's so thoughtful.

I feel so lucky to have found him. Couldn't ask for a more perfect match."

"That's sweet," Anna said.

Callie picked up the phone and stared at the text. Her mouth fell open and she doubled over as a sharp pain sliced through her. "Please, no," came her strangled cry.

Anna rushed to her friend. "Callie, what's the matter?"

Callie held out the phone for Anna to see. The message contained only one word, but it was the one word she never thought she'd see. Especially, not today—a day that had started so well.

SORRY.

"He's gone," Callie whispered, a hollow feeling suddenly engulfing her.

After reading the text, Anna tried to reassure Callie and helped her sit in the chair. "Don't panic. Let me go see what's going on. I'll be right back, okay?"

Callie nodded, but she knew in her heart that today wasn't going to turn out like she thought it would when she woke up this morning. She had been so happy—the birds were singing, the sun was shining and her future with Ethan had looked so bright. Today was supposed to be the first day of the rest of her life with Ethan, or so she thought. She blinked several times trying to stem the tide of tears that threatened to spill down her cheeks. She wanted to be wrong about the meaning of the text, but she knew in her heart that she wasn't.

She racked her brain, trying to make sense of it all. What could have happened between last night's rehearsal dinner and this morning? Ethan had been his usual gregarious self, laughing and talking with the bridal party, her mom and brother and his parents. He gave no hint whatsoever that he was having second thoughts about marrying her. And what about the house? They had submitted an offer for a charming Craftsman style house yesterday. It was perfect for them—three bedrooms, two bathrooms and a modern kitchen. It was her dream house—everything she'd ever wanted with its wide front porch and big back yard. It was where she had hoped to raise their children. Now that was just another ruined dream.

She stood and began pacing, trying to quell her nerves, but nothing seemed to be working. She felt nauseous and the feeling wasn't going away, especially since Anna had not come back right away to reassure her that the wedding was going to happen as planned. She suspected that Anna had guessed the truth when she read the text, but was trying to shield Callie from the awful truth. No one could shield her from this. The only remedy would be if Ethan were magically standing at the altar waiting for her. Then everything would be okay again.

Agonizing minutes passed with no sign of Anna. Finally, her mom, Pat, came into the bridal room. She had tears in her eyes and Callie knew her worst fears had come true. Ethan had left her at the altar.

"Where's Ethan?" she managed to croak out.

Her mother pulled her into her arms for a fierce hug. "I'm so sorry, Callie. Ethan is gone."

Callie stepped back. She didn't want to believe it. "Are you sure? Why would he leave now?"

Pat shook her head. "I don't know, Sweetie. He didn't say anything to anyone. Ethan had slipped outside, and when Shawn went to let him know the ceremony was about to start, he saw Ethan get in the limo. Before Shawn could catch up to him and find out what had happened, the limo drove away."

Callie slumped into a nearby chair. She didn't want to believe the worst, but there was no denying it now. Realizing she still had her phone in her hand, she dialed Ethan's number.

Please pick up. Please. Make this nightmare go away.

It went straight to voice mail. She tried it again, hoping against hope that he'd answer the call. It was not to be and the tears she had held at bay spilled down her cheeks. She felt numb, and like a dam bursting, great sobs wracked her slender frame. "How could he do this?" she cried.

Pat handed her a tissue and rubbed her back. "I don't know what to say, Callie. I just don't know."

Callie looked up at her mother. "What about the guests? And the reception?"

Anna came back into the room and grabbed her friend's hand. "Don't worry about that. Shawn let everyone in the church know that there would be no wedding today. I'll call the Country Club and take care of the details."

Callie nodded. There was nothing left to do except change out of her wedding gown. She reached up and pulled off the veil, tossing it on the chair.

"Let me help you," Pat said.

Callie could barely stand while her mother undid the buttons on the back of her dress. She stepped out of it and Pat hung it in the dress bag.

"Thanks, Mom." A deep throbbing behind her eyes was the beginning of a killer migraine. It was the perfect ending to a disastrous day. She slipped on a t-shirt and jeans. "Can you ask Shawn to drive me home?"

Her mom nodded and slipped out the door. "Be right back."

Within minutes, Shawn was knocking on the door.

"Come in. I'm decent," Callie said.

"You ready?" Shawn asked.

She nodded and another round of tears started when Shawn hugged her.

Shawn hugged her tighter. "Shhh…it will be okay. Come on, I'll take you home."

Callie nodded and grabbed her purse before following her brother out to his car. She slumped in the passenger seat and closed her eyes. The sunlight that had been so warm and friendly less than an hour ago was now her migraine's worst enemy. All she wanted was to crawl into bed, pull the covers over her head, and pretend that this day had never happened.

Chapter 2

*T*OM SULLIVAN COULDN'T HELP BUT smile as his four-year-old daughter climbed up on the white canopy bed. She had grown so much in the past year that she could get into bed without help and she was smart as a whip. She definitely took after her mother on that account. Beautiful and smart Gabriella Sullivan: the most loving wife and doting mother was now just a haunting memory. There would be no more family outings to the park or to the zoo. No more of the birthday parties that Gabby had loved to plan. No more of anything that spoke of Gabby. Had it really been more than a year since his beloved wife passed away? It wasn't fair. Why should a healthy, vivacious, generous woman die at twenty-eight? No one knew the answer. He would never forget that day.

"Tom?"

"Yeah. Hi, Amanda. What's up?"

"You need to get to the hospital."

*Tom stood up abruptly from his drafting table.
"Why, what happened?"*

Amanda's voice cracked. "It's Gabby. She collapsed."

"What do you mean she collapsed?"

*"I don't know, Tom. One minute she was talking,
the next minute she was on the floor grabbing her head.
I'm in the ambulance with her now. We're almost to St.
Vincent's. Come right away."*

*Tom grabbed his car keys and raced out the door.
"I'm on my way."*

*He didn't know what to think as he raced to the
hospital. Maybe her blood sugar was low. She was
always forgetting to eat. Yes, that had to be it. A feeling
of foreboding lingered at the edges of his mind, but he
refused to acknowledge it. No, he wouldn't think the
worst. Gabriella was only twenty-eight. What could
make her faint?*

*He smiled. Gabriella must be pregnant. That had to
be it. They'd been trying to have another child for over a
year without success.*

*His grip relaxed on the steering wheel as he pulled
into the emergency room parking lot. He couldn't wait
to see the look on his beautiful wife's face when the
doctor told her she was expecting. He wasted no time
and hurried to the reception desk.*

*"Hi. My wife was just brought here, Gabriella
Sullivan."*

The young clerk nodded and typed Gabby's name into her computer. "Yes, sir. The doctor is with her now."

"Can I see her?"

"I'll go check. Please wait here."

Tom looked around the emergency room. It was busy, but not overly crowded. There were five other people seated around the room. He took a seat by the sliding glass door and waited. It seemed an interminable amount of time before the clerk reappeared.

"Mr. Sullivan, will you please follow me."

Tom nodded. "How's my wife?"

"I'm not at liberty to say, Mr. Sullivan. The doctor will speak with you and update you on her condition."

Tom wasn't sure he liked the sound of that. He followed her to a curtained off area at the far end of the emergency room. He saw Gabby's best friend, Amanda, sitting in a chair, her face tear-stained. He rushed forward and pulled back the curtain, but Gabby was not there.

"Amanda, what's going on?"

"They took her for a head CT. She was awake in the ambulance and said she had the worst headache she'd ever experienced. Then she lost consciousness. When we got here, the doctor ordered the scan right away."

Tom ran his hand through his hair, more as a nervous reaction than to push back the hair falling into his eyes. "What does he think is the matter with her?"

Amanda shrugged and a fresh round of tears coursed down her cheeks. "I heard one of the nurses say stroke. How can she have a stroke? She's my age. People in their twenties don't have strokes. That's for old people, right?"

Tom took a seat next to Amanda and put his arm around her shoulders. "I don't know, but whatever it is, I'll do whatever it takes to help her through this."

"I know. So will I."

While Tom and Amanda were talking quietly, they heard footsteps coming toward them. Tom stood and looked down the corridor. The doctor was walking toward him, but there was no sign of Gabby.

"Mr. Sullivan, I'm Dr. Whalen. Would you please follow me?"

"Where's Gabby? What's wrong with her?"

"Please follow me and I'll explain everything," Dr. Whalen said.

Tom reached for Amanda's hand. "Come with me."

Amanda nodded and they both followed the doctor down a side corridor to a private room.

Gabriella lay on the bed with her eyes closed. Tom rushed forward and held her hand and gently kissed it. "Sweetheart, wake up. I'm here." He looked at the doctor. "When will she wake up?"

The doctor shook his head and a pained look crossed his face. "I'm so sorry, Mr. Sullivan. Your wife suffered a massive aneurysmal subarachnoid hemorrhage, which means a large blood vessel in her brain burst. The bleeding was extensive. There wasn't anything we could do to save her."

Tom stared slack-jawed at the doctor. "You mean she's dead?"

The doctor nodded. "Yes. I'm so very sorry for your loss."

Behind him, Tom heard gut wrenching sobs from Amanda.

"How could this have happened?"

"We don't know, especially since there's no way to tell how long she had an aneurysm. She could have had it for years."

He stood holding his wife's hand, paralyzed with disbelief. How could Gabby be dead? She had been vibrant and alive just a few hours ago when she kissed him goodbye this morning. He stared at her. She looked like she was merely sleeping. At any moment, she would awaken and give him her special smile, the one that was his and his alone.

"Daddy, can angels make wishes true?" Sophia asked.

Sophia's voice jerked Tom out of his reverie. "What, Sweetie?"

"Can angels make wishes true?"

Tom rubbed his chin. He was always surprised by the questions his daughter asked. They certainly weren't the kinds of things most four-year-olds thought about. "No, I don't think angels make wishes come true, but you know what they can do?"

Sophia leaned closer. "What?"

"They can watch over you and keep you safe."

"Like Mommy?"

"Yes, Sweetie. Just like Mommy. She watches you from heaven and I know she's so proud of you."

Sophia nodded. "I wish Mommy was here."

"So do I, Babygirl. So do I."

Sophia scrunched her hands into little fists and stuck out her lower lip in an exaggerated pout. "Daddy, I no baby. I a big girl."

Tom chuckled. "Of course you are. How could I forget?"

"Is tomorrow liberry school?"

Tom shook his head. "No, not tomorrow. In four more days. Can you show me how many fingers that is?"

Sophia held up four chubby little fingers. "Like me," she proudly exclaimed.

Tom kissed her forehead. "That's right. You're such a smart girl, but it's time for sleep now. Love you, Sophia," he said as she scooted down and relaxed against the pillow. "Here's Puppy," he said, pulling the covers over her shoulders. "Good night."

"Night, Daddy."

Chapter 3

*C*ALLIE PULLED INTO THE DRIVEWAY of her mother's spacious home. The burning bushes along the side of the house had not yet turned a brilliant red and the big maple tree in the front yard was still sporting lush green leaves. The weather was warm for late August, but she knew that could change in an instant. Weather in New England was very unpredictable most of the time. September could bring sweltering temperatures or turn colder if the Canadian air stream drifted too far south. It could snow in October or Mother Nature could be kind and it wouldn't snow until January. She wasn't complaining, though. She loved the changing seasons. Within a month, the trees would be a kaleidoscope of red, orange, yellow and green.

She wasn't looking forward to telling her mom the news. Pat would not take it well, but it was a done deal. It had been nearly five months since Ethan had left Callie at the altar, but the humiliation of that day lingered. Living in a small town had its plusses and minuses, and much to her disappointment, it had become mostly minuses since April. People were awkward around her. They didn't know what to say and Callie was tired of seeing pity in their eyes.

She's the girl that got left at the altar.
What did she do to drive Ethan away?
Who will marry her now?

It was time to move forward with her life and there was no way that could happen if she stayed here.

She steeled herself and got out of the car. There was no time like the present to tell her mom she was leaving town. "Hey, Mom!" she called out as she walked into the foyer.

"In the kitchen," came her mother's voice from the rear of the house.

Tiger, her mom's longhaired orange tabby, met Callie at the door and wove in between her legs until she bent down to scratch behind his ears. "Hey there, big boy. How are you today?" She never tired of running her hand through his soft fur. The cat continued to purr until she stepped away from him. He gave her a look as if to say 'Don't leave yet. You haven't done enough.'

"You're such a spoiled boy," she said, walking toward the kitchen.

She found her mom mixing up a batch of cookies.

"You're making chocolate chip?"

"Yes. The Bridge Club is meeting here tonight and I was specifically asked by Rita to have my famous chocolate chip cookies on hand," Pat said with a chuckle.

"Well, Rita is right. These are the best cookies ever!" Callie leaned over and kissed her mom on the cheek. "Can I sneak a few when they're done?"

"Of course. I wasn't expecting you today. What's up?"

She took a seat at the kitchen island and hesitated a moment before she plunged ahead. The time had come to tell her mom her plans. "I got a new job."

Pat stopped stirring the batter and came around the island to give Callie a hug. "That's wonderful. I didn't know you were looking for a different job. Did something happen at work?"

"No. Not at work, but here in general."

"What? I don't understand."

"Mom, I'm tired of the way everyone looks at me around here. I need a change and I've been offered a job as Children's Librarian in the small town of Bradbury in Vermont."

"Vermont? But, that's so far away."

"Not really, Mom. Maybe five or six hours at most. I can always come back for a visit on long weekends and holidays when the library is closed." She had to stay strong, especially when she saw a hint of sadness pass over her mom's face. She needed a new start and this was the only way she knew how to truly put the debacle with Ethan behind her.

Pat went back to stirring the cookie dough. "I suppose I knew this day was coming. I don't blame you for wanting a fresh start, but I'll miss you, that's all."

"I'll miss you too, but I need to do this."

"When do you leave?"

"I'm moving over the Labor Day weekend."

When her mother didn't say anything more, Callie knew that she was trying to process the suddenness of her departure. She wished there had been another way, but Ethan had taken care of even that timeline as well. She had heard through Anna that he had a new girlfriend, and the last thing she wanted was to accidentally run into them around town. If Ethan wasn't moving, then she had to and she was prepared to do whatever she needed to move on with her own life and forget about him.

"Want some help scooping the dough?" Callie asked.

Her mom gave her a quick smile. "Absolutely, thanks."

Callie reached in the silverware drawer and took out two teaspoons. She handed one to Pat and they went to work scooping the dough on the cookie sheets. When the cookies were in the oven, her mother gave her another hug.

"What's that for?" she asked.

"Just because."

"I love you, Mom."

"I love you too, Callie. I know in my heart that this will be a good move for you. I'm just sad that I won't get to see you as often, that's all."

"How do you feel about packing and moving boxes this weekend?" Callie asked, wriggling her eyebrows.

That got a laugh out of her mom. "Of course. When do we start?"

Chapter 4

"*T*HAT'S THE LAST OF THE boxes," Shawn said, dumping a box in the corner of the living room. "Bobby and I are going to tackle your bed frame next."

"Thank you, guys," Callie shouted from the kitchen of her new apartment. "You're the best ever!"

"I hope this gig includes lunch," Shawn yelled as he plodded down the hall.

Callie looked at Anna and her mom. "Just like a man. Always thinking about his stomach."

Anna chuckled. "Yeah, but he's right this time. I'm starving too."

"How about pizza?"

"Sounds good, but no peppers, okay?"

"Deal. Want to come with me?" Callie asked.

"Sure."

Callie turned toward her mother. "Mom, what kind of pizza do you want?"

"I'm good with whatever you choose," Pat said, emptying silverware into a drawer by the sink. "Want some money?"

Callie grabbed her purse from the counter and said over her shoulder, "No, I've got it. Be back in a few."

Anna followed her out to the car. "There's a pizza place up here? Where? I didn't see it on the way to your apartment."

Callie got in the car and pushed the ignition button. "It's down one of the side streets," she said, while buckling her seat belt. "I only saw it because I was looking at a cute little yarn shop on the corner."

Anna buckled her seat beat. "Really? A yarn shop? I want to see that. I wonder if it's open on Sundays."

"No idea. Let's check it out while we wait for the pizza. We might not get a chance tomorrow."

"Sounds good to me," Anna said.

It took ten minutes for Callie and Anna to reach the quaint downtown. It was a typical New England town with a park boasting a gazebo and mature trees in the town center. Abutting the park was a white church with beautiful stained glass windows on one end, a Town Hall building across the street, and a number of shops plus a couple of restaurants on the opposite side of Main Street. It was a Hallmark picture postcard in the making.

Callie flipped on her blinker and turned right on Spencer Street. "Look, that's the little shop I was talking about," she said, pointing to her right.

"Awesome."

Callie quickly found a parking space and the girls walked the two blocks back to the pizza shop. A little bell sounded as they went inside.

"Oh, this is so cute," Callie said, looking around the small restaurant. There were ten tables, each adorned with a red-checkered tablecloth and a vase of flowers. The menu featured hot sandwiches in addition to a good combination of pizza choices.

"Hi, can I help you?" a young man behind the counter asked.

Callie walked up to the counter. "Hi. I'd like to order three large pizzas. One cheese, one pepperoni and one Hawaiian."

"No problem. We can do that."

"Can you let me know the total?"

"Hold on. Let me get that for you."

Callie waited while he rang up the sales on the cash register.

"That will be $28.50 all together. Will you need drinks with that?"

Callie pulled out a twenty and a ten from her wallet and handed them to him. "No. We're all set on drinks."

"It will be about twenty-five minutes."

"Perfect. We'll be back, thanks," Callie said. She turned toward Anna. "Ready to check out the yarn shop?"

Anna nodded. "Let's go. I can already envision new scarves and mittens for Christmas this year."

"You got that right. I suspect I'll have plenty of time on my hands."

"Maybe, but you could meet someone new, too. You should at least keep an open mind to the possibility."

"I know, but I'm not sure I'm ready to plunge back into the dating scene. Learning a new job will be enough for the moment."

"I understand, but you never know. Just keep an open mind, okay?"

Callie chuckled. "Do you know something I don't?"

Anna shook her head. "Not at all. Life has a way of throwing you curves, that's all."

Once inside the yarn shop, Callie pulled out her phone. "I better set an alarm for twenty-two minutes or we might lose track of time. My brother will never forgive me if we don't come back with hot pizza."

Anna chuckled. "Good idea. We know how we get— like little kids in a candy store."

The girls tackled the bins of yarn first. It was Anna's mom who had taught them to knit and crochet when they were young and they both took to it easily. Crafts had been one of their shared passions throughout their years of friendship.

The shop was a knitter's paradise, with a variety of baby yarn, variegated yarns and mohair skeins. Anna picked up a light blue mohair skein and rubbed it against her cheek. "Oh, this is so soft. This one is definitely going home with me."

"What are you making with it?"

"Scarf for my mom," Anna said.

"She'll love it. I'm going to get some of that soft gray for my mother. It will complement her winter coat perfectly."

"Have you seen the books on the wall over there?" Anna asked, pointing to the front corner of the store.

Callie walked over and began looking through the books on crocheting. Her phone beeped while the sales woman was ringing up her purchases. "Wow, just in time. We need to keep these bags in my trunk until my Mom goes home, okay? I don't want her to see them."

"Good idea," Anna said as they walked back to the pizza shop.

Callie went inside and picked up the pizza. "Smells delicious," she told the young man behind the counter. "Thank you."

"Enjoy," he said. "Hope to see you again."

"Okay, let's go back," Callie said. "My stomach is growling too."

By the time the girls returned to the apartment, Pat had found the box of dishes and glasses and had set the kitchen table. Shawn and Bobby were already seated and waiting on lunch.

"Hope you're hungry," Callie said as she and Anna came through the front door.

"Starving," Shawn said.

"So what else is new?" Callie said, planting a kiss on her brother's cheek. Shawn was two years older, but they'd always been close and had plenty to talk about, especially when it came to their love for fantasy and science fiction books. They'd spent more hours than they could count discussing their favorite authors and what they would have done differently if they were the ones plotting out the story.

As everyone took a slice of their favorite pizza, Callie looked around the apartment. From the kitchen, she could see all the way to the front door. She was glad she'd found an apartment with more of an open-concept, so when she did entertain, she wouldn't be stuck in the kitchen cooking while her guests were chatting in another room. The kitchen was fairly modern, with plenty of cabinets and a gas stove that Callie loved. It was open to a large living room/dining room space. Her furniture fit nicely into the space and the whole apartment was flooded with natural light that would be welcome, especially in the dreary winter months. Her bedroom, which was a decent size, and the bathroom were down a short hallway.

"This is delicious," Shawn said, grabbing another piece of pepperoni pizza.

Bobby nodded while reaching for a piece of Hawaiian. "So, why way up here in Bradbury?" he asked.

"I needed a change," Callie said, not elaborating further.

Bobby nodded, clearly understanding what she was referring to. Everyone in town seemed to know about Ethan leaving her at the altar.

"Plus, it's the only place that offered me a position," she said, chuckling.

After lunch, Shawn and Bobby moved furniture around until Callie was happy with its placement. While the guys helped Callie, Anna and her mom started unpacking the rest of the kitchen boxes.

"Are you sure you're happy with everything now?" Shawn asked. "I don't know when I'll be back up here, so make your requests now."

Callie walked through the apartment again. Her bed would only fit against one wall, so there were no other options with that room. There was only room for her dresser so her desk was in the corner of the living room. "Can you hook up the computer and printer before you leave?"

Shawn nodded. "Is the cable hooked up already?"

"The cable guy is supposed to be here today, although I don't know what time."

"Okay. I'll get everything plugged in, but you're going to need a splitter."

"A what?"

"A splitter so you can have a connection for your television and your computer from one cable wire. Make sure both connections work before the guy leaves."

"Have I told you you're my favorite brother?"

Shawn laughed. "I'm your only brother!"

After another hour, Shawn, Bobby and Pat were ready to leave.

"Thank you all so much for helping today," Callie said. She hugged each in turn.

Pat held on longer. "I'll miss you, Sweetie."

"I'll miss you too, Mom. I'll try to come home as soon as I can."

Pat nodded, blinking back tears. "Sounds good. Love you. Bye."

"Love you too. Bye."

Callie watched them drive away before turning back to Anna. "Well, guess I'm really on my own now."

Anna nodded. "It'll be good for you, and if you really hate it up here, you can always move back next year when your contract is up."

"I know, but I'm hoping I love it. I need some space, you know?"

"I do."

The girls talked and unpacked boxes long into the night.

Chapter 5

*C*ALLIE TOOK A DEEP BREATH before opening the library doors. She smoothed down the invisible wrinkles in her black slacks and tugged on the sleeves of her cashmere sweater. Anna had stayed with her two extra days after Pat and Shawn left, and between the two of them, they had finished setting up the apartment and emptying all the boxes. It looked like she'd been living there for a while and even her clothes were ironed and hung up in the closet.

This was what she wanted—a new start away from everyone—but now that she had it, she wasn't sure she'd made the right choice. She was alone in a new town with a new job looming ahead of her. What if the job didn't work out? She'd be stuck here for a year before she could move again or else pay a hefty fine for breaking her lease. Would she make new friends? It was hard to know the answers, but she was determined to put her best foot forward. It was time to start the next chapter in her life.

She clamped down her fear and realized she was excited to start her new job as Children's Librarian. The library was housed in a historic brick building not far from the town center and she had no problem finding it. The sun was shining and there wasn't a cloud in the sky. Seemed like a good omen to start her new life.

She pulled open the heavy oak door and stepped through. The inside of the library did not match its exterior. It was a modern oasis, totally opposite from the charm of the quaint looking downtown. Off to her left, there were a dozen workstations lined up in the center of a large room with tables and chairs hugging both walls. It looked like the perfect place to study and research school projects.

Directly in front of her was the reception desk. The wood and glass desk was sleek and stylish. Callie walked toward it.

"May I help you?" a young woman asked.

"Hi. I'm Callie Spencer," she said, extending her right hand. I'm the new Children's Librarian.

"Oh, hi. I'm Susan Dobson. Nice to meet you," she said, grasping Callie's hand in a firm handshake. "The director is expecting you. I'll show you to her office."

"Thanks so much. I'm really looking forward to working here."

"Good. We're all happy you're here," Susan said as she climbed the stairs to the second floor.

When they reached the top of the stairs, Callie noticed the row of offices to her right, but it was the large children's area that piqued her interest. Warm sunshine spilled through the bank of windows, giving the room a cheerful feel. There were low bookshelves on three walls and it looked like there was a good selection for the children to choose from. There were also a number of kid-sized tables and chairs. In the far corner, there was a comfy looking rocking chair glider. It looked perfectly situated for reading stories to expectant little faces.

"What a great space," Callie said.

"Yes. The kids love it. You'll see soon enough. We have Library School Story Time every Tuesday and Thursday at ten a.m. for the little ones and an activity class at two-thirty for the older children," Susan explained. "Mary's office is just down here." Susan knocked on the door before sticking her head inside. "Callie Spencer is here."

"Good. Show her in," Mary said.

"Thanks again, Susan," Callie said as she went into the director's office.

"My pleasure. Talk to you soon."

"Callie, welcome," Mary Reading said.

Callie extended her hand in friendship. "Thank you. I'm happy to be here."

Mary shook her hand. "Please, sit down. Would you care for coffee or tea?"

Callie shook her head. "No, I'm fine. Thank you."

"I want to go over a few details with you about today's itinerary for the Children's Library. Nothing too elaborate, but there is a schedule we like to keep to, especially with the younger children. Their attention spans begin to wane after thirty minutes or so. It's best if the activity changes to re-engage them once again."

"That sounds good."

Mary and Callie talked for forty-five minutes before they emerged from the office. "Let me show you where the selections are for Story Time. If the children want a certain book to be read, feel free to choose that one instead. A couple of our youngsters are quite vocal in their selections."

"Sounds like fun."

"Oh, they are. You'll see for yourself in about fifteen minutes when the ten o'clock group comes in."

Callie had finished picking out the three stories for Story Time when she heard pounding feet behind her.

"I'm Sophia! It's liberry time."

Callie stooped to Sophia's level. The little girl was adorable, with dark ringlets flowing to her shoulders and deep brown eyes that sparkled with excitement. "Hello, Sophia. I'm Miss Callie. Are you excited to hear stories today?"

Sophia nodded enthusiastically and plopped herself down not far from Callie's rocking chair. "I'm ready."

Callie chuckled. When she stood, she came face-to-face with the most handsome man she'd ever seen—like

'Statue of David' handsome. Her eyes traveled from his toned chest, past his chiseled jaw line to the most sparkling blue eyes she'd ever seen. To complete the picture of perfection, his wavy hair curled around his ears and brushed against his shirt collar. Her jaw fell open. It was like being hit with a bolt of lightening, not that she knew what a bolt of lightening felt like, but this had to be close. Butterflies roiled through her insides and her self-confidence fled. When he gave her a slow and sexy smile, she felt weak in the knees.

"Hi. I'm Sophia's father, Tom Sullivan. My daughter can get a bit enthusiastic about things, as you can see from her greeting."

Callie nodded. "So I see," was all she could squeak out. How does one talk to a walking god? She had no idea, but she had to pull herself together.

Tom stood in her sightline a moment longer before he moved to the back of the room.

Callie followed his every move. She couldn't get enough of him.

What an idiot I am? I have a Master's Degree in Library Science and the best I can come up with is 'So I see.' Oh, boy, how lame.

She shook her head to dispel the cobwebs that seemed to have invaded her brain, rendering her a blithering idiot. Just in time, as more children began to arrive. She smoothed down her sweater and plastered a smile on her face.

I'm a professional. I can do this. Tom will see I can string two sentences together; that is, if he stays in the Children's Room. What if he leaves?

Tom didn't leave and Callie greeted the children and their mothers. Most of the mothers stayed, but a few slipped away for some quiet time downstairs.

She took a deep breath. It was time for Story Time to begin. She looked at each of the children sitting in a circle, waiting on her. "Good morning, boys and girls. I'm Miss Callie, the new Children's Librarian."

"Good morning, Miss Callie," came a chorus of voices.

She sat in the comfy chair and picked up the first book. "Today's story is *Mr. Brown Can Moo. Can you?*" she began, reading to the group of six children. Sophia sat directly in front of her. "Are we ready?"

Six little heads nodded as she turned to the first page.

"Oh the wonderful sounds he can do! He can sound like a cow. He can go MOO, MOO.

The children eagerly joined in with a chorus of "Moo, moo!"

"He can sound like a bee. Mr. Brown can BUZZ. How about you? BUZZ, BUZZ."

Sophia was quick to repeat buzz buzz.

"He can sound like a cork. POP, POP, POP, POP. He can sound like horse feet. KLOPP, KLOPP, KLOPP."

After each new page, the children enthusiastically repeated the sound.

"He can sound like a rooster...COCK A DOODLE DOO."

Callie was having as much fun as the children. Their laughter was infectious, but her eyes kept stealing a look at Sophia's father. Tom was standing off to the side. She saw him chuckle a few times and his smile made her pause. It was like a refreshing drink of water after surviving a trek across the desert. He probably had no idea how he was affecting her and she could hardly believe it herself. One day on the job and she was going gaga over one of the parents? This was silly. She had to stop acting like a schoolgirl with her first crush. She didn't even know if Tom was available. He could be married. Plenty of dads are taking responsibility for childcare these days. She turned her attention back to the kids and finished the book with a flourish.

Six little pairs of hands clapped.

"Can you read it again?" one of the children asked.

Callie looked at each of them. "Well, if you all want to..."

A chorus of yeses sang out and she wasted no time in rereading *Mr. Brown Can Moo. Can you?*

After the reading of several more books, Story Time was over. Mothers claimed their children, some stayed and read more stories, while others said they'd be back on Thursday for the next session. At last, only Tom and Sophia were left.

"You did a wonderful job today. You're so good with the children," he said.

"Um…thank you. I enjoyed it myself. Sophia is a smart little girl."

Tom nodded. "Indeed she is." He looked to his left, where his daughter was picking out books to take home. "She's been reading for a few months now. God help her kindergarten teacher next year."

Callie chuckled. "I'm sure she'll do fine." She wanted to talk with him all day. His voice wafted over her like her favorite violin music. It was strong, yet subtle and she wanted nothing more than to listen to the sound of his voice.

"Callie," he said. "Would you—"

"Daddy, I found them," Sophia said, running up to her father with an armload of books.

"Sorry, looks like I've been summoned to check out," Tom said. "I guess we'll see you Thursday, then."

Callie nodded, trying hard to hide her disappointment. "I'm looking forward to it. See you then. Bye."

Would I what? she wondered as they left. What was Tom going to ask her? Maybe, join him for coffee sometime? Dinner? Her answer would have been a resounding yes. She definitely wanted to get to know the hunky guy with the velvety voice. She watched him take Sophia's hand and head down the stairs. She'd have to wait until Thursday to see him again. It was going to be a long two days.

Chapter 6

*T*OM TIGHTENED HIS GRIP ON Sophia's hand as they descended the stairs. She was bounding down each step and he didn't want her to fall. "Easy, Sophia. Not so fast."

"I can do it, Daddy."

"I know you can. I just want you to be careful, okay?"

Sophia nodded and jumped down from the last step into the lobby. They went to the counter and checked out her books.

"Okay, time to go home," he said. "I've got work to do and Miss Julie is coming over to watch you."

On the drive home, he couldn't get the new librarian out of his mind. Callie was funny and vivacious; a knockout with her long luxurious hair and beautiful green eyes. He was captivated by the sprinkle of freckles across her nose. She was the first woman to pique his interest in a long time. He had wanted to ask her out for lunch, but Sophia's timing as usual was impeccable and he never got the chance. It didn't matter. He was determined to ask her out on Thursday. He very much wanted to get to know her better.

Mary had mentioned to him last week that she had hired a new Children's Librarian, but he hadn't given it much thought. The last couple of librarians had been older women who were warm and friendly, and he had assumed the next one would be older as well. It was a pleasant surprise when he had walked into the Children's Room today. He would have to thank Mary for her excellent taste in Children Librarians.

He looked in the rearview mirror and saw his daughter attempting to read one of her new books. "Sophia, we have to stop at the grocery store before we go home."

"But, Daddy. I want to read my books."

"I know you do and you'll get a chance later on. We need to get some things for lunch so you and Miss Julie will have something to eat. Do you want to help me pick out the fruit?"

Sophia nodded and Tom chuckled. Going grocery shopping was not high on his daughter's list of fun things to do. He tried to make a game of it—counting how many apples and bananas they bought, but Sophia wasn't fooled. Every other aisle, she asked if they were done yet. Next time, he'd shop while Julie was watching her.

By the time they got home, it was nearly lunchtime. Julie had pulled into the driveway just ahead of them, and Tom was glad they hadn't made her wait. She got out of her car and helped Sophia out of her booster car seat.

"Hi, Sophia."

"Miss Julie, I have new books. We can read them."

"Of course we can, but first we're going to have lunch. What did Daddy buy?"

"Chicken," the little girl said as she marched up the walkway. "He always buys chicken."

Julie chuckled and followed her. She slipped the key in the lock and pushed open the door. "Can you put your books in the family room?"

"Okay," Sophia said, skipping down the hall.

Tom followed them inside and put the bags of groceries on the counter. "Hey, Julie. How are you today?" he asked the older woman.

"Good, although I don't think Sophia is impressed with your choice for lunch."

"I know, but we were running late and I just grabbed the first thing I saw."

Julie began unpacking the bags. "Not to worry. I'll whip up something she'll enjoy."

Tom patted her shoulder. "Thank you so much. Have I told you lately what a godsend you are?"

It was Julie's turn to chuckle. "It's my pleasure. Sophia is like my first grandchild. Goodness knows when Kim and John will have a child."

"Well, I'm happy you're here. I'll be in my office if you need me. I have to finish up a couple of drawings today."

Julie nodded. "I'll call you when lunch is ready."

"Thanks," Tom said, walking out of the kitchen and down the hall. He heard Sophia asking Julie if she could help. Even though she had grumbled about chicken for lunch, she couldn't resist trying to help prepare it.

He settled at his desk and clicked open the Auto Cad LT software on his computer. He had two renderings that were due at the end of the day. One needed only minor tweaks, but the other would need a solid two hours of work to finish. He had finished the first project and emailed it off to the client when Julie called him for lunch.

"Be right there," he shouted. He got up and stretched. As if on cue, his stomach rumbled. As he made his way to the kitchen, the tantalizing aroma of Julie's famous stir-fry tickled his nose. How did she do it? Whenever he attempted to duplicate the dish, it fell short by a long shot. He didn't fancy himself a chef, but neither he nor Sophia had starved in the last year. That was something, at least.

"That smells delicious," he said, sitting at the kitchen table.

"Daddy, I helped," Sophia said, grinning from ear to ear.

"You did? Then that's why it smells so good. I bet Miss Julie was happy you pitched in," he said with a chuckle, stealing a look at Julie.

"She was a big help," Julie said. "Now eat up before it gets cold."

"Don't have to tell me twice."

He had only taken a few bites before Sophia started telling Julie about Miss Callie. She was clearly taken with the new librarian and, frankly, so was he—her quirky smile, the way she scrunched up her nose, and her infectious laugh as she read to the children. She was a rare beauty. He wondered what had brought her to this little town. Whatever it was, he was going to take advantage of it. He daydreamed about kissing her sweet lips and running his fingers through her hair. What if she smiled just for him?

"Daddy, you no listen."

"What?"

Julie rescued him from his daydreams. "Sophia was telling me how much she likes Miss Callie at the library."

"Yes. We did indeed like her." He saw Julie raise an eyebrow, but she didn't say anything further and neither did he.

Chapter 7

*I*T SEEMED AN ETERNITY BEFORE the Thursday morning Story Time rolled around. Callie stood in the Children's Room, waiting with bated breath to see if Tom Sullivan came with his daughter. She had thought of little else but seeing his handsome face again. This time, she wouldn't be caught off guard and hoped to prolong their conversation. The easy relationship he had with his daughter endeared him even more to her. She had always loved children and couldn't imagine herself marrying a man who didn't love kids.

What?

Marrying him?

What on Earth am I thinking? I haven't spoken ten words to the man and I'm already thinking about marrying him?

Slow down, girl. Start by having a conversation with him first.

"Miss Callie," came a joyful cry.

Callie glanced over to the stairs and saw Tom and Sophia heading her way.

Now be cool.

Say something witty.

Don't stand there like an idiot.

Sophia ran up and hugged her legs. "I missed you," the little girl said.

She patted Sophia's back and gave her a quick squeeze. "I missed you too. I'm so glad you're here for Story Time." When she lifted her eyes, Tom stood in front of her, a mere twelve inches away. His chiseled features and intense eyes captivated her. A lump formed in her throat and all she could get out of her mouth was, "Hi."

His blue eyes seemed full of mischief, and he gave her a lopsided grin. "Hi, yourself."

She struggled to think of something else to say, but her mind was a total blank. What was it about Tom that turned her into a quivering mess? A mess that wanted to beg him to kiss her—kiss her long and deep while she ran her hands through his hair. Now that would be a proper hello.

Think.

Come on, you can do this.

I'll ask him out for coffee. Yes, that's not too forward.

Callie opened her mouth to ask Tom out for coffee before her courage died, but it was at that moment that Head Librarian Mary walked into the Children's Room.

"Oh, good. I see you two have met," Mary said, standing next to Tom.

"Yes. We actually met on Tuesday," Tom said.

Mary squeezed Tom's arm and began pulling him away. "Can I steal you away for a few minutes? I need you to look at the latest drawings. I think there's something off, but I can't put my finger on it."

"Sure, happy to take a look."

Callie watched him walk away and sighed. Again, she'd shown herself to be an aficionado of words. 'Hi,' was all she had managed to utter. Yes, that tantalizing tidbit of conversation would certainly keep her in the forefront of his thoughts all day. She couldn't imagine what he thought of her. What had happened to all those witty things she thought of on the way to work today? Somehow, thinking about what she wanted to say and actually saying it to Tom when he stood in front of her was not the same thing. Definitely not the same thing. That sexy smile, his rich baritone voice that strummed against her skin like a fine-tuned instrument, and a body that begged to be touched were too much for her to process while trying to be witty at the same time. Maybe if he wore a bag over his head, she'd remember her witty lines.

"Miss Callie," came more little voices, interrupting her thoughts.

Callie shook her head to dispel her daydreams of Tom Sullivan. It was time to get back to business. "Good morning, Sally, Timmy and Amanda."

The children all took their seats on the floor, with Sophia once again sitting directly in front of her.

Such a beautiful child, Callie thought. *I wonder where her mother is? Is Tom divorced, separated? Might be good to find out before I embarrass myself by asking him out.*

"Are you all ready for Story Time?"

"Yes," the children said in unison.

"Good. Today is extra special. After our story, we're going to make Halloween decorations."

The children cheered and Callie dove into reading the first story. She was in her element and delighted the children with the different voices the story called for. As she read, she stole looks around the room, but Tom had not reappeared. With the story finished, she asked the children to take their seats at the table. There were orange construction paper pumpkins, crayons and stickers at each seat. She was totally engrossed with helping the children color their pumpkin faces when she felt someone behind her.

"Those look good."

She turned around and found Tom behind her. She swallowed hard and was determined not to miss another opportunity to talk with him. "Hey there. Aren't they doing a good job?"

Tom nodded and glanced over at Sophia's pumpkin face. His daughter was hard at work making a scary face, although the end result was actually adorable.

"Daddy, look at mine," Sophia said, holding up her pumpkin.

"Wow, you're doing such a good job, Sweetie."

The little girl beamed and went back to work with her black crayon.

Tom touched Callie's arm. "May I talk with you a moment?"

Callie's heart rate went into overdrive. She wondered if he could hear the pounding in her chest. "Sure."

They moved over to the side of the room. Callie held her breath, anticipating what Tom wanted to talk about. Was he going to ask her out?

"So, I was wondering if you'd like to have lunch with me sometime," Tom said.

Callie gave him her prettiest smile. "Really?"

"Yes, really. I'd like to get to know you better, but if you'd rather not, I understand. It occurs to me I never thought to ask you if you were involved with anyone."

Callie nodded. "No."

"No? Is that no, 'I'm not involved with anyone' or no, 'I don't want to have lunch with you?'"

Callie chuckled. "The former and I'd love to have lunch with you. Thank you." She watched as Tom exhaled. Had he been holding his breath waiting for her answer?

"I wanted to ask you on Tuesday, but Sophia's timing kind of spoiled that," he said with a chuckle. "She'll be with the sitter tomorrow, if that's not being too pushy."

"Not pushy at all. Lunch tomorrow will be great."

"Miss Callie, I need your help," little Amanda cried.

"Excuse me, I'm being paged," Callie said. She hurried over to the table, smiling from ear to ear.

"Of course," Tom said, wearing his own smile. He hadn't been able to stop thinking about Callie since he met her and was looking forward to having lunch with her. He wanted to know everything about the delicate beauty. Before he left the library, he made sure to get Callie's phone number so he could text her the directions to the restaurant.

***

Callie licked her lips as she checked the GPS. The restaurant Tom had chosen for their lunch date was less than two miles away. When she had asked Mary if she could have a few extra minutes for lunch, Mary had been most agreeable, especially when Callie told her she was meeting Tom. Now that she was almost there, her nerves were in overdrive. She wasn't sure she would be able to eat, especially with the butterflies doing summersaults in her belly.

She pulled into the parking lot of the diner, found a parking spot and made her way inside.

"Can I help you?" a kindly older woman asked.

Callie nodded. "Yes, I'm meeting someone for lunch."

"Oh, you're meeting Tom?"

"Yes. How did you know?"

The woman winked. "I'm Sally and he told me to look out for the prettiest girl to come through the door. Come this way. He's already seated."

"Oh, really?" Callie said.

The hostess looked over her shoulder. "I've known Tom for years. Really nice guy."

Callie smiled. "Good to know."

"Here we are," Sally said.

Tom stood. "Hi. I see you found the place all right."

"Yes. GPS worked fine," Callie said. She sat down in the booth and her eyes drank in the male specimen known as Tom Sullivan. He probably had no idea how sexy he was, and when he smiled, he lit up the world around him.

"Would you care for something to drink?" Sally asked.

"I'd like a diet Coke, please," Callie said.

"And you, Tom? What can I get for you?"

"I'm good with the water, thanks."

"Be right back," Sally said.

Callie tried to think of something to say. Once again, she found herself tongue-tied in Tom's company. What was it about him that unbalanced her so much? It was more than just his good looks, even though they were outstanding. He touched something deep inside her. She instinctively knew that Tom was different from most men. "How's Sophia?" It was the only thing she could think of.

"She's good. Spending the day with her sitter, Julie."

"That's good. She's such a sweet little girl." Callie's nervousness was getting the better of her and she picked up the menu to stop the babbling that threatened to escape her lips. That was her safety mechanism whenever she was nervous—talk nonstop about nothing in particular. She didn't want to do that today.

"The food here is very good," Tom said. "I've personally tried almost everything on the menu."

Callie looked up. "Really? What do you suggest?"

"The grilled chicken sandwich is good or the Cobb salad is excellent," he said.

Sally appeared at their table and put the diet Coke in front of Callie. "Do you need a few more minutes?"

Callie shook her head. "No. I'm all set. I'll have the Cobb salad, please."

Tom nodded. "And I'll have the same. Thanks, Sally."

"Okay. Two Cobb salads coming up," she said, taking their menus.

"Well, I don't know about you, but I'm a little nervous. Haven't been out on a date in a very long time," Tom said.

Callie giggled. "Same here. I'm sitting here racking my brain, trying to say something witty. Nothing comes to mind."

Tom reached for her hand. His touch sparked something inside her and her nervousness was replaced by a longing she hadn't known she had. She had shut down emotionally after Ethan, and with a simple touch, Tom had brought her back to life, chipping away the ice around her heart. His hand was warm. "I'm very glad you asked me out for lunch," she said.

"It's my pleasure. Enrolling Sophia in Story Time was the best thing I've done in a long time."

"I'm glad you did too." Callie felt the heat rise up her cheeks. Tom seemed to know exactly the right thing to say. Was he the real deal? She wasn't sure, but was willing to give him a chance and find out.

Chapter 8

*T*OM LAUGHED AS CALLIE TOLD another story about growing up with her older brother, Shawn. She clearly adored him. He'd never seen a brother and sister so close and it gladdened his heart to see such family love. Even though he'd just met her, he knew Callie was special. Her smile was pure sunshine and the more time he spent in her company, the more he wanted.

Their salads were long gone, and she was reaching for her wallet. "No need for that. This is my treat," he said.

A sweet smile lit up Callie's face. "Thank you, Tom. I had a lovely time, but I'm sorry, I have to go. Duty calls, you know?"

Tom nodded. "Indeed I do," he said, picking up the bill.

They walked to the front of the diner and Tom paid the bill, leaving Sally a generous tip. "Thanks, Sally. Lunch was great as usual," he said.

"Glad you enjoyed lunch. Come back again soon," Sally replied.

Tom and Callie went outside and walked to her car. "I really enjoyed lunch," he said.

"So did I. Next time it's my treat," she said, opening the car door.

"Next time?" Tom said, arching an eyebrow.

Callie stopped short. "Oh, that's if you'd like there to be a next time. I apologize if I assumed too much."

Tom let out a rich baritone laugh. "I'm just teasing you. I'd love to see you again."

Callie smiled. "That's good. I'd like to see you again too. When are you free?"

"Would you like to come for dinner tomorrow night?" he asked.

"To your house?"

"Yes, that's the general idea. Sophia will be there, if you're nervous."

"I'm not nervous, and yes, I would love to join you and Sophia for dinner. Text me the time and the directions."

Tom's gaze lingered on her soft sensual lips as she spoke. He wanted to feel them pressed against his own, but didn't want to be too forward. He'd been out of the dating game for years and wasn't sure what women expected these days. If she leaned forward for a kiss, he wouldn't say no, but he wasn't going to initiate it, not yet, anyway. When she didn't make a move toward him, he said, "Will do. I'll see you tomorrow. Bye, Callie."

"Bye." She slipped inside her car, put on her seatbelt, and gave him a friendly wave before driving off.

Tom watched until the car disappeared from view. His spirit was soaring. What was it about this woman? He hadn't felt like this in such a long time. He had stepped through the other side of his grief and it was time to start living again, not only for his sake, but for Sophia's as well. Callie made him want be happy again.

There was a spring in his step as he walked to his car. Once inside, he inhaled sharply. *What am I going to serve for dinner? I doubt seriously if Callie would like a box of macaroni and cheese.*

He pulled out his phone and called Julie, explaining his dilemma. "Okay, good. I got it. I'll pick up everything on my way home."

Crisis averted. Tom had known Julie would have a favorite recipe to share. Chicken parmesan didn't seem that hard to make. His skill at cooking wasn't that of a master chef, that was for sure, but he'd give it a try. As backup, he'd corral Julie before she left tomorrow and ask her to go over the recipe once more.

CALLIE WORE A SMILE on her face the whole way back to the library. She was on cloud nine. Tom wanted to see her again. She could hardly believe her good fortune that he was interested in her. She certainly wasn't looking to date anyone when she moved up here, but there was something about Tom that captivated her. His strong, but gentle, presence intrigued her and she couldn't wait to see him again.

Their lunch together had been a little nerve-racking in the beginning, but once they started sharing childhood stories, they settled into an easy and fun conversation. After lunch, she'd thought Tom was going to kiss her in the parking lot. She had lingered a moment, but he didn't move to close the gap between them. She was momentarily disappointed, until she thought about how special their first kiss would be when it finally happened. Maybe tomorrow night after dinner would be the night they connected. She could hardly wait to kiss his very kissable lips.

She pulled into the library parking lot and found a space at the back. Grabbing her purse, she flung open the car door and raced into the library. She hadn't realized how late she was getting back from lunch and hoped her supervisor wouldn't be angry with her. It was only her first week on the new job, and already, she'd exceeded her allotted lunch hour by nearly an hour. Time had gotten away from her. As she climbed to the top of the stairs, she spotted Mary in the Children's Room trying to help a harried mother find a book a cranky little girl wanted.

"Can I be of help?" Callie asked.

Mary looked up. "Yes, I'm sure you'll know which is the right book. I can't seem to find the correct one."

Callie bent down to the crying girl and wiped the tear from her face. "Don't worry. I'll see if I can find your book, okay?"

The little girl nodded and said, "I want fish book."

Callie looked at the mother for clues. "Any ideas?"

The young woman ran her hand through her hair, shaking her head. "I don't know. I thought she wanted the Dora book. We looked at them all, but evidently none of them are the right one."

"I have an idea," Callie said. She went to various bookshelves and began pulling out a few different books. She brought them over to one of the tables and motioned for the little girl to join her. "What's your name, Sweetie?"

"Joy."

"What a pretty name. No more tears now, okay? Want to look at these books? Is your fish book here?"

Joy's eyes lit up when Callie put *One fish, Two fish, Red fish, Blue fish* by Dr. Seuss in front of her. "Fish book," she screeched, grabbing the book. "Mommy, fish book."

Joy's mother clapped. "Yay! Let's go and check it out."

Joy nodded and happily made her way to the stairs with her grateful mother in tow. The frazzled woman mouthed "thank you" to Callie as they went downstairs.

Callie picked up the other books she had pulled from the bookcases.

"You're so good with the children," Mary said, taking one of the books from Callie to help reshelf it.

"Thanks. It's usually a matter of trying to figure out what they're trying to say. That poor mom looked like she was at her wit's end. I'm glad I guessed right."

Mary nodded. "Me too. So, how was lunch?"

"It was wonderful," Callie said, looking away, a blush staining her cheeks pink.

"That's nice."

"I didn't realize how long I was gone. Time just slipped away."

"No problem. Do you plan on seeing Tom again?"

Callie's head snapped back toward her supervisor. She had moved away from her childhood home to distant herself from everyone knowing her business. Now, here it was happening again. "Why?"

Mary reached out and grasped her hand. "Forgive me, Callie. I don't mean to be pushy. Bradbury is a small town and everyone knows the trauma that Tom went through when his wife died. It was so tragic. I guess I'm a little over-protective of him, that's all."

"His wife died? How?"

"Brain aneurysm. There was nothing the doctors could do. She died before Tom made it to the hospital."

Callie swallowed hard. "That's awful. When did that happen?"

"Let me think. It had to be a year ago last July. I think that's right. I know Gabby died in the summertime, just not sure what month it was. The whole town came out for the funeral. Everyone loves Tom. He's such a good guy and you're the first woman he's shown any interest in dating. So forgive my intrusion earlier. I guess I need to curtail my own curiosity."

"No, it's fine. I don't mind telling you. In fact, I'm happy to share that I really like him too. He asked me to dinner tomorrow night."

"Fantastic. I'm glad you two are connecting."

"Thank you, Mary. I'm sorry I overreacted. I moved away from home because of everyone prying into my life and I thought it was happening again. Now that I know the circumstances, I'm glad people are looking out for Tom."

Mary nodded. "So, did something happen to force you to move?"

Callie nodded. "You could say that. I was left standing at the altar."

"Oh, you poor thing. Come into my office and I'll make some tea. You can tell me all about it. It must have been terrible for you."

"Worst day of my life," Callie said, following her supervisor down the hall.

Chapter 9

*C*ALLIE STOOD IN THE AISLE looking at the bottles of wine lined up like little soldiers on the shelf. Not being a wine drinker herself, she had no clue which one to select for her dinner with Tom. She didn't want to go to his home empty-handed, but now that she was here, she was at a loss what to choose, especially not knowing what he was serving. Should it be red or white? Pinot Grigio, Sauvignon Blanc, Chardonnay, or perhaps something red, like Pinot Noir? She debated a while longer before she chose a bottle of Sauvignon Blanc and one of Pinot Noir. Couldn't hurt to bring both.

Her hands shook a bit as she paid for the wine. She didn't know whether it was nerves or excitement. The only thing she knew for sure was that she would get to spend more time with Tom. She programmed Tom's home address into her GPS. It turned out to be not too far from the liquor store. Her mind wandered as she drove to his home. Would he kiss her tonight? Maybe she would kiss him instead. What if he didn't like her being so forward?

So many thoughts and questions swirled around her mind with no answers in sight. Before she knew it, she was parking in front of Tom's stately colonial.

The home was painted white with black shutters. A walkway leading to the front door was lined with neatly trimmed boxwood shrubs on either side. Along the front perimeter, azalea bushes were abundant. Callie could picture the blaze of color when they bloomed in the spring. They would be breathtaking.

She took a deep breath. It was now or never. She grabbed the bag of wine, got out of the car, and headed for the front door. She rang the bell and immediately heard Sophia's voice.

"Me get it, Daddy." The door opened and Sophia stood there with a smile that stretched from ear to ear. "Miss Callie is here," she yelled.

"Hi, Sophia," Callie said. "May I come in?"

Tom's frame filled the doorway. "Of course," he said, opening the outer glass door. "Hope you didn't have any trouble finding the place."

Callie shook her head. "No trouble at all." As she stepped inside, Sophia hugged her legs. She stroked the little girl's head. "I'm happy to see you, Sophia."

Sophia looked up. "Want to read?"

"Maybe later, okay?"

"Sophia, let Miss Callie come in," Tom said, gently pushing his daughter out of the way.

"I brought wine," Callie said. "I wasn't sure what you were serving, so I have a red and a white. I hope you like wine."

Tom reached for the bag. "Thank you and yes, I do like wine. We're having Chicken Parmesan tonight, so the white will be perfect."

Callie followed Tom into the kitchen. It was a good-sized room with a large center island. The island itself could seat five people. The room boasted beautiful maple cabinets and stainless steel appliances. It was a chef's dream kitchen. She wondered if Tom was the chef or if it was his late wife who had designed the space. Not wanting to be rude, she didn't ask.

There was another eating area in front of the bay windows overlooking the back yard. Three place settings had already been set up.

"I helped Miss Julie," Sophia said, running into the kitchen.

"You did?"

Sophia nodded, clearly proud of herself.

Tom chuckled. "Guess my secret is out. I had a bit of help with dinner."

"It smells delicious."

"Sophia, can you get a box of pasta from the pantry?"

She nodded and headed toward pantry door. "I got one," she said as she ran back to them. "Here, Daddy."

Tom took the box and turned to Callie. "I hope you like linguini?"

"Yes, I do. Thanks."

The dinner was a smashing success. Callie couldn't remember the last time she'd enjoyed a meal as much. Sophia told her all about her kitty, Sam, who they had adopted from the local shelter. Sam, it seemed, preferred Sophia's bed as his favorite sleeping spot.

"Sam doesn't like kisses," Sophia said.

"Want to know a secret?" Callie asked.

Sophia nodded.

"If you scratch behind his ears, he'll love that."

Sophia seemed to consider what Callie had said. "Okay," she said. "I try." She got off the chair and ran down the hall toward her bedroom.

Callie helped bring the dishes to the sink. "That was delicious."

"I'm so glad you enjoyed it," Tom said. "Care for more wine?"

"I think I'll wait a bit. I did promise Sophia I'd read with her."

"That's nice of you."

"She's such a sweet little girl," Callie said, bringing the sauce bowl to the sink.

"Thank you. She certainly has taken a shine to you."

Standing this close to Tom, Callie felt butterflies starting their hectic dance in her insides again. He exuded sex appeal while rinsing off dishes, which she hadn't thought possible, and she longed to feel his strong arms around her.

Sophia came bounding back into the kitchen. "I found one, the unicorn one," she said, holding up her book.

Callie turned toward her. "Oh, that sounds like a good one."

"Why don't you two go on into the family room while I finish up here?"

Sophia grabbed Callie's hand. "I show you."

Callie chuckled. "Lead the way."

After three stories and a game of Candy Land, Sophia was tucked into bed for the night. Tom poured them fresh glasses of wine and they sat on the couch in front of a fire in the family room.

"She's usually not so hard to get to bed," he said.

"Sophia was fine. I enjoyed playing with her."

Tom handed her a glass and took his own. "A toast then. To a nice quiet evening," he said, tapping her glass.

Callie's heart hammered inside her chest. This moment was what she had been waiting for since their lunch a few days ago—to be alone with Tom, to feel his lips pressed against hers and to feel his arms around her. She took a sip of wine, never taking her eyes off him.

"I'm so glad you're here," Tom whispered, putting his glass on the coffee table. He ran his finger along her jaw line. "There's something special about you, Callie. I knew it the first time I saw you." He took her hand and brought it to his lips, kissing it gently.

Callie felt tingles down to her toes. The connection with Tom was more than she had ever experienced before. "Thank you." She put her glass down. "You're pretty special yourself."

Tom leaned in and brushed his lips against hers. She parted her lips and his tongue explored her mouth. As their kiss deepened more, she could feel the heat between them. She was being swept away in a sea of endless waves of passion as their bodies melted into one another. When Tom broke away, she felt adrift without his strong presence touching her.

"Wow," was all she could say.

Tom rewarded her with a megawatt smile. "Wow, yourself. You're so—"

An agonizing scream broke their intimate moment. Tom jumped up and raced down the hall toward Sophia's room. Callie was quick on his heels. She saw him scoop up the little girl. "Shhhh…" he whispered in her ear. "Daddy's here now. It's okay." Sophia quieted while Tom gently rocked her back and forth in his arms.

"I'm going to go. Sophia needs you," Callie whispered.

She saw Tom look at her. "Sorry," he whispered.

"It's okay, really. I'll talk to you soon. Thank you again for dinner." She turned away and grabbed her purse on her way out.

Driving home, she relived Tom's kiss over and over again. What had he been going to say before Sophia's nightmare interrupted him? She wondered if he felt their connection as strongly as she had. The kiss had been incredible, the most sensual and passionate kiss she'd ever shared with another man, including Ethan.

She definitely wanted to see more of Tom and enjoy more of his kisses. She reached into her purse and dug out her phone. Scrolling through Contacts, she tapped Anna's number. She hoped she didn't catch her friend sleeping, but she had to talk to someone about Tom. Anna would understand.

"Hello," answered a sleepy voice.

"Anna, did I wake you?"

"Callie, hi. Guess I fell asleep watching this stupid movie. What's up?"

"If you want to go back to sleep, I'll call you tomorrow."

"No. It's fine. I'm awake now."

"Good, because you're not going to believe this. I've met someone."

Callie heard her friend gasp.

"You what? Already? You've only been up there a few weeks. See, didn't I tell you to be open to the possibility?"

Callie giggled. It was like their girlhood conversations about boys. "I know. It just kind of happened. He's the father of one of the children who attend Story Time."

"Really? Is he divorced?"

"No. Actually, he's widowed. Anna, you should see him. He's gorgeous and oh man, can he kiss."

"He kissed you already?"

"Oh, yes, he did and quite well at that."

The two young women continued their conversation about hunky Tom Sullivan long after Callie arrived home.

Chapter 10

THE WEEKS FLEW BY WITH a series of lunches and dinners with Tom and Sophia, as well as a healthy dose of Tom's soul-searing, curl-your-toes kisses. She had never felt such a connection with anyone as she had with Tom. Callie was falling hard for him and she believed he felt the same way about her.

Their romantic dinners together sparked such passion in her that she didn't want the evenings to end. She could listen to the sound of his voice for days on end and never tire of it. What was it about this guy that spun her carefully "I'm done with men" world totally upside down? There was no tension or angst, almost a weekly occurrence when she had been with Ethan, and it was absolute bliss not to have to worry about saying the wrong thing. She hadn't realized how tense she had been until she was out of that toxic situation. Ethan leaving her at the altar was the best thing he could have ever done for her, although at the time, she thought she'd never recover from the heart-wrenching pain of his betrayal.

Callie spent hours on the phone talking with Anna about Tom and Sophia. Anna had been cautious at first, especially since she feared Tom was Callie's rebound guy, but the more Callie told her about him and his young daughter, the more Anna realized how happy she was in his company. Sometimes love just finds you, no matter what the circumstances are.

Tonight, she was going over to Tom's for dinner and a pumpkin-carving session. Halloween was in two days, so they couldn't put it off any longer. She could hardly wait to see him again. He had not brought Sophia to Thursday's Story Time and she was sorely disappointed. He had called her at lunch to explain that Sophia had a mild fever and he thought it best to keep her at home.

The day slowly crawled to quitting time. At five o'clock, Callie retrieved her coat and purse from the library's little kitchen area and headed out. She stopped by Mary's office to wish her a good night.

Mary nodded. "Have fun tonight."

"Thank you. I will. See you on Monday."

Callie hopped in her car for the short ride over to Tom's home. She hoped Sophia was feeling better. Carving pumpkins was so much more fun with children around, especially someone as precocious as Tom's daughter. Within fifteen minutes, she was pulling her car into the driveway and walking up the manicured walk.

She rang the doorbell and waited. Sophia's high-pitch squeal sounded almost immediately and she heard the tiny footsteps running toward the door.

"Miss Callie is here," Sophia said, opening the heavy oak door.

"Hi Sophia. Are you feeling better today? I missed you at Story Time yesterday."

Sophia nodded as Callie opened the glass door and made her way inside.

"Hey there, in the kitchen," Tom's voice floated down the hall.

"Daddy has a big knife," Sophia said, grabbing Callie's hand.

"Well, let's go see what he's up too, shall we?" She closed the front door and walked down the hall to the kitchen with Sophia skipping alongside her. She stopped short in the doorway, her attention focused on the older woman standing in the kitchen with Tom.

Tom walked to her and kissed her gently on the lips. "Hi, you. I want you to meet my Mom, Jane Sullivan."

Jane walked forward with her hand outstretched. "Hi, Callie. It's a pleasure to meet you at last. Tom has told me so much about you."

Callie shook Jane's hand. "Uh, oh. Was he complaining again about my skills at Candy Land? I've won five games in a row and he's won zero. Even Sophia can beat him."

"I win too," Sophia chimed in.

Jane laughed. "Well, I can see why Tom is so smitten with you."

Callie smiled. "It's nice to meet you, Mrs. Sullivan."

"Please, call me Jane."

Tom wrapped his arm around Callie's waist and gave her a loving squeeze. "Well, now you've gone and done it. A Candy Land challenge has been issued!"

"Why don't you all sit while I get dinner on the table? Then we can carve the pumpkins."

"Thanks, Mom," Tom said. He turned to Sophia. "Go wash your hands for dinner, okay? Do you want some help?"

"No, me do it," the little girl said as she ran to the hall bathroom.

"Something smells delicious," Callie said. "Anything I can do to help?"

Jane shook her head. "No, I've got it covered. It will be ready in five minutes."

As Tom and Callie walked to the table, she leaned in and whispered in his ear. "Why didn't you tell me your mom was coming over tonight?"

"I didn't want you to be nervous. Besides, I knew she'd love you."

"You know me too well. I would have been nervous if you had told me."

"See, I knew it!"

Sophia came bounding back into the kitchen. "All done."

They sat while Jane brought baked stuffed chicken, mashed potatoes, corn and dinner rolls to the table.

"I hope you're hungry, Callie. Oh, you're not one of these young women who eat a mere three bites before pushing your plate away, are you?"

Callie shook her head. "No, ma'am. As Tom can attest, I have an excellent appetite. This smells absolutely delicious."

"Good. Tom, will you do the honors and carve the chicken?"

Tom stood and picked up the carving knife. "Sure. Now who wants what?"

The meal was a resounding success and, while Jane and Callie cleared the table, Tom spread a sheet of plastic on the floor and brought the pumpkins inside. He proceeded to cut out the stem on each one. "Everyone ready to carve their pumpkins?" he asked.

"Sure are," both Callie and Jane said in unison.

"Daddy, I want one too," Sophia said.

Tom patted her head. "Of course you do. See, I cut off the stem and now we have to scoop out the inside before we can cut out the face." He handed her a spoon. "Here you go. Dig in and scoop it out."

Sophia did her best to get the pumpkin out, but in the end, Tom had to help her. Callie and Jane joined in the fun and scooped out the insides of their own pumpkins.

"Lots of pumpkin pie and seeds from these," Jane said.

Although no one said out loud that it was a competition, Jane, Tom and Callie each worked hard to carve the best face. In the end, they had to admit that Tom had done the best. Callie's pumpkin had a lopsided grin and Jane's pumpkin had eyes of different sizes.

"Well, I suppose I have to give you this one. After all, I don't want you pouting any more about being beaten at Candy Land," Callie said.

Tom chuckled. "I see the gauntlet has been thrown down on this one. Just wait until we dig out that board again," he said, his eyes sparkling with delight.

It was Callie's turn to laugh. "You're on!"

"Sophia, will you help me take these out to the front porch?" Jane asked.

The little girl jumped up and down. "I can help."

"Yes, you can." Jane handed her one of the smaller pumpkins. "Hold tight now." Jane's arms were full of the other three pumpkins. "Be right back."

Once they were out of the room, Tom held Callie's face. "Have I told you how beautiful you are?" He leaned in and kissed her, gently at first before deepening the kiss. When they broke apart, he said, "Finally. I've been dying to do that all night."

"You do have a way of making my heart flutter," Callie whispered. "I've missed you. Story Time wasn't the same without you."

"I've missed you too. Before Sophia comes back, I wanted to ask if you'd like to go Trick or Treating with us on Sunday."

"Oh, I'd love too. What time?"

"How about five o'clock?"

"Perfect. I can't wait to see Sophia in her princess costume," Callie said.

Sophia came running back into the kitchen. "Daddy, I helped Nana."

Tom scooped her up in his arms. "You're such a good helper," he said, kissing her apple cheeks.

By the time Jane went home and Sophia was tucked in for the night, Callie couldn't wait to once again feel Tom's lips pressed against hers. She couldn't get enough of his touch—the way he caressed her cheek or ran his finger along her jaw line down to the hollow of her neck or the way he kissed her. There was no doubt about it, she was falling in love with him. Was it possible to know with absolute certainly that this was the person you wanted to spend the rest of your life with after such a short time? She fantasized what life with Tom would be like, waking up in his strong arms every morning and nights of passionate lovemaking.

Passionate lovemaking?

Am I really thinking about this so soon?

She heard his footsteps as he came down the hall after tucking Sophia in bed. Finally, some alone time.

He poked his head in the family room. "Would you like a glass of wine?"

"Yes, thank you."

In less than a minute, he was sitting beside her on the couch with a bottle of wine and two glasses in his hands. He pulled out the cork and poured them each a generous glass. "To a wonderful night spent with my favorite girl," he said, clinking her glass.

"To a wonderful night."

He leaned forward and kissed her. "Yum. You taste so good."

"You're not so bad yourself," she said and was rewarded with a megawatt smile.

"My mother loved you, by the way. Of course, I knew she would."

"I was surprised to see her here."

Tom caressed her check. "You forgive me for not warning you?"

"Yes. Your mom is awesome. I really liked her too."

Callie leaned back and studied the gorgeous man sitting beside her. It was time she took a leap of faith. If she didn't, she'd regret it for the rest of her life. "Tom, speaking of moms, I was wondering if you and Sophia would like to come home with me for Thanksgiving. I know my mom and brother would love to meet you."

"How can I say no to my favorite girl? I would love too, but if we spend Thanksgiving with your family, we must spend Christmas with mine. Deal?"

Callie smiled. "Deal."

Tom held her in his loving gaze before he brushed his lips against hers. "You mean the world to me and I do believe I'm falling hopelessly in love with you."

It was more than Callie could have hoped for. "Well then, I guess we're even then, because I'm already hopelessly in love with you."

Tom took their wine glasses and set them on the coffee table before pulling her into his arms. "My darling Callie," was all he said before he captured her lips.

Chapter 11

THE TEN O'CLOCK STORY TIME hour was over and Tom walked toward Callie, who was putting the books back on the shelves. "We're all packed. I'll pick you up at three. Okay?"

Callie nodded as Mary came out of her office.

"Hi, Tom," she said, giving his arm a friendly squeeze.

"Hi, Mary. I was going to pop in to your office to wish you a Happy Thanksgiving. Are all the kids coming home?"

Mary shook her head. "No, Caroline has been invited to meet her new beau's parents, but the boys will be here. I'm sure they'll bring home piles of laundry. Somehow washing machines don't work on campus."

Tom chuckled. "Guilty as charged. I did the same thing to my poor mother. Always a bag of laundry whenever I went home."

"It's the way of boys, I think."

"Indeed," Tom said.

Mary turned to Callie. "There's no need for you to stay any longer. I'll cover the Children's Room. I seriously doubt if we'll get any more little visitors today, especially since the two o'clock session has been cancelled."

"Really?" Callie asked.

"Yes. Now scoot out of here, but I want the details of the visit, you hear?"

Callie laughed. "Of course. Wouldn't dream of keeping anything from you." She turned toward Tom. "Looks like I'm a free woman. I just need to go home and grab my suitcase."

Tom kissed her. "Sounds good. We'll follow you to your apartment. Sophia, are you ready to go visit with Miss Callie's mom?"

The little girl jumped up and down. "Yay."

"Happy Thanksgiving, Mary," Callie said as they walked toward the stairs.

"Happy Thanksgiving. Have a safe trip."

"Thank you."

AFTER NEARLY SIX HOURS in the car, they were finally pulling into her mom's driveway. Callie looked in the back seat, where Sophia was still sleeping. "She did well being in the car for so long."

"Yes. She's usually pretty good, but this is the longest trip we've ever taken. Thank goodness I remembered to load up the iPad with some movies. Not sure how many more verses of 'Old MacDonald' I could stand."

Callie chuckled. "I know, but at least we're here now. Should I wake her?"

Tom shut off the car and unlocked the doors. "I'll get her. She may not wake up if I carry her into the house. I'd rather wake her up inside."

"Okay. I'll grab the suitcases."

Pat was at the door and held it open while they all came inside.

Callie put the suitcases down and hugged her mother. "Hi, Mom. So good to see you."

"I missed you, Sweetie. I'm happy you're here."

Callie eased out of her mother's embrace. "Mom, this is Tom Sullivan and his daughter, Sophia."

Tom nodded. "I'd like to shake your hand, Mrs. Spencer, but mine are a little occupied at the moment."

Pat chuckled. "Please, call me Pat. Come in. Come in. No need to stand around in the foyer."

They followed Pat into the kitchen. "You guys must be famished. I've made lasagna for dinner." She turned toward Tom. "Tom, I hope you like Italian."

Tom nodded. "Love it, actually. Thank you for allowing Sophia and I to join you for Thanksgiving."

"No need for thanks. I'm happy you're here and, of course, Sophia too."

The mention of her name seemed to wake Sophia. She opened her eyes. "Daddy?"

Tom kissed her cheek. "It's okay. Remember I told you we were going to visit Miss Callie's mom?"

Sophia nodded and tried to sit up in his arms. "Daddy, me down."

Tom eased her to the floor. "Can you say hello to Mrs. Spencer?"

Sophia hugged his legs and peered at Pat. "Hello."

Pat knelt down so that she was eye-to-eye with the little girl. "Hi, Sophia. I'm so happy you're here. Are you hungry?"

Sophia nodded.

"Good. I think we could all use some dinner. Why don't you lead everyone to the table over there? Can you do that?"

Sophia grabbed Tom's hand. "Come on, Daddy," she said, dragging him to the table.

"Mom, I'm just going to take the suitcases upstairs. I'll be right back."

As Callie walked back to the foyer, the door opened and in walked Shawn. "Shawn!" she said, nearly flinging herself into his arms, hugging him fiercely. "I didn't know you were coming over tonight. I thought I'd see you tomorrow."

"Ma called me and said she was making lasagna. You bet I'm here."

"Awesome. We just got here ourselves. Come, I want you to meet Tom."

"Great."

"Look what the cat dragged in," Callie said as they walked back into the kitchen.

Shawn kissed Pat's cheek. "Hi, Mom. Smells delicious in here."

"Glad you could make it. Go have a seat."

Tom stood when Shawn appeared. "Hi. I'm Tom Sullivan and this is my daughter, Sophia."

Shawn shook his outstretched hand in a firm handshake. "Good to meet you. I'm Shawn."

Sophia tugged on Tom's pants. "Daddy, where's Puppy?"

"It's probably still in the car. I'll get it," Callie said.

Tom handed her his keys. "Thanks."

"No problem," she said, turning on her heel. "Be right back."

She hit the remote twice and heard the locks click before opening the back seat door. Sophia's little white dog, if that's what you could still call it, was on the floor. The stuffed animal had definitely seen better days. The dog's fur was nearly rubbed off on one side of its face as if she had kissed it bare. "She loves that little dog." She grabbed the dog, and as she went to close the car door, she heard footsteps in the driveway.

She looked up and her heart did a stutter step inside her chest. Walking with purpose toward her was Ethan.

Oh, no. He's the last person I want to see today, or any day, for that matter. What could he want?

"Callie, I was hoping I'd find you here," Ethan said.

Callie crossed her arms across her chest. She steeled herself as a sinking feeling settled into the pit of her stomach. "What do you want, Ethan?" He tried to reach for her, but she stepped back. "Don't touch me. What do you want?"

"Don't be like that, Callie. I just want to talk to you, that's all."

Callie burned with anger. "Talk? You want to talk to me? Now, after seven months?"

Ethan looked down, admonished by her words. "I'm sorry. I made a huge mistake leaving you at the altar. I want to make it up to you," he said, pulling a ring box out of his pocket. He opened it and her former engagement ring sparkled in the sunlight. "How about we forget what happened last spring and start again? What do you say? Will you marry me?"

"I say you have one hell of a nerve coming here." She felt a presence behind her and felt Tom's strong arm around her waist.

"Is there a problem?" Tom asked.

She saw Ethan look between her and Tom before he snapped the ring box shut. "Who's this guy?"

Before Callie could answer, Tom said, "I'm her fiancé and I don't take kindly to you upsetting her."

Callie stood, stunned into silence—fiancé? Was Tom just saying that to get rid of Ethan? Or was there a proposal in the works? All the anger she felt a moment ago evaporated in an instant. She didn't know if Tom wanted to marry her or not, but the way he stood beside her made her heart soar.

"We're done here, Ethan. You should leave," she said.
"Callie."

"You heard the lady," Tom said. "You're not welcome here."

Ethan glared at Tom before he turned on his heel and stormed off.

She took Tom's hand and together they walked back into the house. "Thank you for that. He was the last person I ever thought I'd see in my mother's driveway."

Tom tipped her chin up and kissed her lips. "No problem. I'm here anytime you need me."

"What took you so long?" Pat asked.

"Ethan was in the driveway begging for a second chance," Callie said.

Shawn jumped up. "I'm going to kick his ass."

Pat grabbed his arm. "Shawn, language please. There's a little girl sitting here."

"Oh, sorry, Ma." He looked at Sophia. "That was bad language. Sorry, little one."

"Don't worry. Tom took care of him," Callie said.

"Good. Now let's all sit down to eat before the food gets cold," Pat said.

Chapter 12

*A*s THE WEEKS FLEW BY without any sign of Tom proposing, Callie chalked the whole incident at Thanksgiving up to Tom doing his best in getting rid of Ethan. She tried hard not to be disappointed, but if she was honest, she'd been hoping that Tom would propose while they were at her Mom's house. The more time she spent in Tom's company, the more she realized that he was the man of her dreams. He was kind and considerate and oh-so-sexy. His kisses seared her soul and left her breathless. She could imagine a wonderful life they'd share together. She sighed just thinking about it.

Sophia's voice brought her back to the present: "Miss Callie, look at mine."

Callie looked at her construction paper Christmas tree. "Sophia, that's so pretty. Good job." She went around the table and complimented all the children on their designs. She had pre-cut the trees out of green construction paper before the children had arrived and had a variety of stickers for each of them to choose from in decorating their trees. "Everyone has done such a good job. Are you ready for the star topper now?"

A chorus of yeses echoed around the table.

As she handed each child a gold star, she spotted Tom out of the corner of her eye. She gave him her prettiest smile and was rewarded with one of his in return. She handed the last child the star topper. "Okay, children. That's all for today. I won't see you again for a few weeks. Don't forget your Christmas trees." Thursday was Christmas Eve and there was no Story Time scheduled until January. "I hope Santa brings you exactly what you want."

One by one, the children gave her a hug and wished her a Merry Christmas.

Tom peered at Sophia's project. "Nice job, Sophia."

The little girl beamed. "Miss Callie gave me stickers."

"I can see that. Shall we put it on the refrigerator when we get home?"

Sophia nodded. "I want to."

"Didn't she do a good job?" Callie asked as she stood next to Tom.

"Yes, she did." Tom wrapped her in his arms. "Hello, you," he said before kissing her soundly on the lips.

She melted into his arms.

"Are you ready to meet the Sullivans?" he whispered in her ear.

"The Sullivans?" she asked.

"My mom called and told me all three of my brothers are coming for Christmas this year."

"Really? Maybe I shouldn't come, then. I don't want to intrude on your family get-together."

He kissed her again. "Don't be silly. You're not intruding at all."

"Well, if you're sure."

Tom hugged her tightly. "I'm absolutely sure."

CALLIE PARKED OUTSIDE JANE Sullivan's home. Her stomach was in knots. It was one thing to meet Tom's mother, but quite another to meet his brothers. What if they didn't like her? What would she do? The last thing she wanted was to create a wedge between Tom and his family, but she couldn't imagine giving him up either.

She took a deep breath. "It's now or never," she said, grabbing the two apple pies she had baked yesterday. It was her mother's recipe and was a favorite whenever she made it. She rang the doorbell and waited.

She could hear the screech of children's voices. It sounded like they were having fun.

It was Tom who opened the front door. "Merry Christmas!"

"Merry Christmas," she said. "Hope I'm not too early."

"Your timing is perfect. It's a zoo in there. Are you ready?"

Jane came to the door. "Hi, Callie. Merry Christmas, dear," she said, kissing her cheek.

"Merry Christmas, Jane. Thank you for inviting me to your home. I hope I'm not intruding on your family visit."

"I'm so glad you came and you're not intruding at all. Here, let me take those," Jane said, reaching for the pies.

Once his mother had walked away, Tom swept Callie in his arms and kissed her passionately. "I'm so glad you came. Come on in and meet everyone."

Tom led her into the kitchen. It opened up to an expansive family room. There was a nine-foot Christmas tree in the corner and toys and children were scattered about the large room. "Hey, everyone," he said. "This is Callie." He put his arm around her waist and gave her a reassuring squeeze. "Callie, meet everyone."

Callie laughed and gave the group a wave. "Hi." She was a little overwhelmed by all the people, but Tom held onto her.

"Hey, Tom, are you standing there for a reason?" one of his brothers asked.

Tom pointed up. "Hmmm…look at that."

Callie looked up. They were standing under a bouquet of mistletoe.

Tom took her hand and knelt on one knee.

Callie was speechless, and the butterflies began roiling inside her stomach.

Was he going to propose?

Now?

In front of everyone?

"Callie, there aren't enough words to tell you how much you mean to me. You've brought life and love back into my life and I never want to let you go. Would you do me the great honor of becoming my wife?"

Tears of joy flowed down Callie's cheeks. This was what she had been hoping for since Thanksgiving. She had no idea Tom had been planning this. "Yes, yes, yes!" she said.

Tom reached into his pocket and pulled out a ring box. He opened it to reveal a beautiful two-carat emerald-cut diamond.

Callie's hand flew to her mouth. The ring was exquisite. "Oh my god, that's beautiful!"

Tom took it out of the box and slipped it on her ring finger. "There. That's perfect." He stood and swept her up in his arms. "You've made me the happiest man in the world," he said, kissing her.

Everyone began clapping and crowded around the happy couple. "Congratulations," they said.

"Now that you've said 'yes,' let's get married tomorrow," Tom said.

Callie looked at him. "What? We can't get married tomorrow. I have to call my Mom and Shawn and tell them our happy news."

"There's no need," came a voice from the crowd. Pat, Shawn, Anna and her mother all stepped forward. "We're right here."

Callie ran to Pat and hugged her. "Mom, I'm so happy you're here, but how did you know?"

Shawn spoke up. "Tom discussed it with us at Thanksgiving. We've been ironing out the details ever since."

"So, when you told Ethan I was your fiancé, you were already planning this?" she asked.

Tom nodded. "Yes, and I almost ruined the surprise."

"But I still can't plan a wedding in a day," Callie protested. "I don't even have a dress."

Jane spoke up next. "I think you'll find nothing is impossible when it comes to the Sullivan family. Follow me. We have another surprise for you."

"Another one?" Callie asked. "I don't know how many more surprises I can handle."

All of the women followed Jane down the hall to one of the bedrooms. When she opened the door, Callie inhaled sharply. Hanging on a dress rack were five exquisite wedding gowns for her to choose from.

Anna took her hand. "Come on. Let's look at them."

Callie turned toward Jane. "How did you do this?"

Jane chuckled and pointed to one of the older women crowding into the room. "This is Pam, one of my oldest and dearest friends. She owns the bridal shop two towns over. Your mom and Anna gave her some suggestions of your taste and she brought these for you to choose from.

Callie found it hard to find her voice. "Thank you, Pam. I'm at a loss for words."

"If you don't like any of these, we can go to the store and look at more," Pam said.

Callie turned back to the dresses. They were all stunning, but she immediately went to the strapless chiffon gown. It had a beaded and crystal belt at the waist, but no other embellishment. It was absolutely perfect. She picked up the hanger. "This is the dress."

"Are you sure?" Pat asked. "Do you want to try them on?"

"No, Mom. I don't need to. I can tell it will fit. This dress is stunning."

"Would you like to pick a veil?" Pam asked. "I brought a selection."

Callie shook her head. "No, thank you. I'm going to skip that." She held the dress against her. "This dress is so perfect, it doesn't need one."

"Are you ready to make a few more decisions?" Jane asked. "Will Anna be your maid of honor?"

Callie put the gown back on the rack. "Of course! She's my dearest friend. I can't imagine getting married without her."

Anna rolled another dress rack to Callie. "Here are bridesmaid's dresses. Pick anything you like."

Callie looked through the dresses and stopped at the emerald green chiffon. "Oh, this is so pretty. Do you like it?" she asked Anna.

"I knew you'd pick that one," Anna said.

"You did?"

"Yes. We've been here a few days and I've tried on all of these. The minute I saw the green one, I knew that was the one."

Callie looked from face to face. "I can't believe you guys did all this."

"It was actually Tom who organized everything," Jane said.

"He did?"

Jane nodded. "When he gets something in his head, there's no stopping him."

"This is just incredible," Callie said.

"Shall we go see what else my son has in store for you?" Jane asked.

Callie nodded. Pat and Anna each took one of her hands.

"This is so exciting," Anna said. "Are you surprised?"

"Surprise doesn't even cover it. I'm stunned."

"You have no idea how hard it was to keep it a secret, but I swore I would," Anna said.

The women rejoined the men and Callie walked to Tom. "You planned all this?"

He smiled. "I did. I don't want to wait any longer to share my life with you."

"But what about a venue, the marriage license, the—"

He placed a finger across her lips. "Got it all covered." He pointed across the room. "See that guy? He's the mayor and will open Town Hall for us tomorrow morning so we can get our marriage license."

"He will?"

"Yes. This is what's so wonderful about living in a small town. The minister at the Congregational Church will marry us."

"I don't know what to say," Callie said.

"All you need to say is yes and I'll take care of everything else."

Callie threw her arms around Tom's neck. "I love you so much."

"And I love you, my darling sweet Callie."

The rest of the day was a whirlwind of activity. Callie spent the afternoon getting to know Tom's three brothers. Only one of his brothers was married. Derek and Kerry had two children and a third child on the way. A daughter would join two older brothers in the spring. The afternoon was filled with good food, good conversation and plenty of laughter.

As the evening wound down, Tom pulled Callie into his arms. "I think you need to get some sleep. We have a big day tomorrow."

Callie kissed him. "Thank you for being so wonderful."

He held her gaze. "Anything for you, my love." His mouth captured hers and he kissed her long and deep before letting her go. "I'll come by tomorrow at ten and we can go to Town Hall."

"Okay. See you then."

Callie went in search of her mom and Anna. She found them in the family room talking with Derek and Kerry. "Looks like I'm being sent home," she said with a chuckle.

"I'm going to stay with Jane," Pat said. "You and Anna go spend some time together."

"You sure, Mom?"

"Yes. I'll see you tomorrow."

Callie gave her a hug, said her goodbyes, and left with Anna in tow. Once they were in the car, she turned to her best friend. "I can't believe this is happening."

"Your fiancé is very focused and doesn't want to waste another day without you."

Callie stared at her ring. "I'm just stunned. Tom is everything I could ever want. I feel like I'm living in a dream."

"No dream. It's really happening and I couldn't be happier for you."

Callie squeezed her friend's hand. "Thank you for being here."

"Wouldn't be anywhere else. Now let's get home so you can get some sleep. Can't have the bride with dark circles under her eyes, now can we?"

Chapter 13

*T*HE NEXT DAY, TOM PICKED Callie up at her apartment and they drove to Town Hall. The mayor was waiting for the happy couple.

"Morning Tom, Callie," he said.

Tom shook his hand. "Thanks, Rick. I really appreciate you doing this."

"No problem. Let's get this done."

It took less than an hour to fill out the paperwork and they walked out of Town Hall with a marriage license. Tom drove her back to her apartment. "See you soon," he said.

"Can't wait."

Callie and Anna spent the next few hours giving each other a manicure, pedicure and doing hair and makeup.

"Okay, you can look now," Anna said.

Callie opened her eyes. "Oh, Anna. It's perfect." She turned her head to see the braids Anna had woven into both sides. She had pulled the rest of Callie's hair to the side and used the curling iron to put in long curls that spilled over her shoulder.

"You look beautiful."

"I couldn't do it without you. I'm so happy you're here."

"Are you ready to go? I'm sure your mom wants to help you get dressed."

"Absolutely. Let's go."

The scene at Jane's house was controlled bedlam. With five women all trying to get ready, every mirror in the house was occupied.

"We're here," Callie called out.

"In the kitchen," Jane said.

Callie and Anna entered the kitchen. Jane and Pat were sitting at the island sipping coffee. "Oh my. You girls look beautiful," Jane said.

Pat stood and hugged her daughter. "You're beaming. I love seeing you so happy."

"I am happy, Mom. I've never felt like this before. I know Tom is the man for me."

"Good. We sent the guys and the children to the church."

"What about the reception?"

"Don't worry. Everything has been taken care of. All that's left to do is for you to get dressed. The limo will be here in thirty minutes."

Callie went over and hugged Jane. "Thank you for everything—for opening up your home, for arranging all this, and most of all, for your amazing son."

"You're welcome, Callie, but it's you who have put the light back in Tom's eyes. I have something for you." She reached for a small jewelry box sitting on the counter. "I would be honored if you'd wear these for your 'something borrowed.'"

Callie opened the box and revealed stunning pearl and diamond earrings sitting in blue velvet. "These are perfect," she said, hugging her soon-to-be mother-in-law. "Thank you." Tears welled in her eyes at the outpouring of love from Tom's family. "I feel so blessed to be part of the Sullivan family."

Both Jane and Pat wiped tears away. "No tears. You'll ruin your makeup and we can't have that. Let's get you dressed," Jane said.

By the time everyone was ready, the limo was waiting in the driveway. "Time to go," Jane said.

"What about the flowers? I totally forgot about a bouquet."

Jane chuckled. "Not to worry. The flowers are waiting for you in the limo."

Once inside the limo, Callie opened the box containing her bridal bouquet. Her mouth fell open as she looked at the all-white bouquet of roses and mums with a green ribbon woven throughout. "It's beautiful."

Anna opened her box to reveal a bouquet similar to Callie's, but with lavender ribbon. "So pretty."

It didn't take long to drive to the church. Shawn and Sophia greeted them as the limo drove up to the front door. Shawn opened the door and helped Callie out.

"Miss Callie is here!" Sophia shouted. "Daddy said you're my new mommy now."

Callie bent down and kissed her cheek. "Yes, I am."

The little girl threw her arms around Callie's neck. "I love you."

Callie hugged her tight. "I love you, too. Are you ready to be a big girl and walk down the aisle?"

"I have flowers," she said, holding up her little white basket of flowers.

"They're beautiful."

"Hey, Sis," Shawn said. "You look beautiful."

"Thank you," Callie said, hugging her brother before going inside the church.

"It's show time! I'm walking the two moms down the aisle and I'll be right back." He held out his arms to Jane and Pat. "Ready?"

They both nodded and Shawn escorted them to the front of the church.

"Sophia, are you ready?" Anna asked.

The little girl nodded.

"I'll be right behind you."

Shawn opened the church doors and Sophia and Anna made their entrance. Camera flashes went off all the way down the aisle. Everyone stood in anticipation of the bride's appearance.

"You ready?" Shawn asked.

"Absolutely," Callie said, squeezing his arm.

As they walked down the aisle, Callie was amazed at all the guests filling the church. It looked as though the entire town had turned out for their wedding. Her heart filled to overflowing with happiness, especially since her handsome husband-to-be waited for her at the altar with a smile that stretched from ear to ear.

"Wow," Tom said when Shawn placed Callie's hand in his. "You look exquisite."

The minister began, "Dearly beloved, we are gathered here today to join in holy matrimony this man and this woman."

The minister blessed their rings. "Tom and Callie have written their own vows. Tom, do you take Callie to be your lawfully wedded wife?"

"I do." He picked up the diamond band and slipped it on Callie's finger. "Callie, you mean the world to me. Before you came into my life, I was adrift without an anchor. With your beautiful smile and generous spirit, you captured my heart and gave me what I had been searching for. I love you with every fiber of my being and promise to spend every day making you happy."

"Callie, do you take Tom to be your lawfully wedded husband?"

"I do." She picked up the platinum band and slipped it on Tom's finger. "Tom, when I moved to Bradbury, I never thought to find the man of my dreams. I love your strength, your gentleness, and most of all, I love the way you make me feel. You fill my heart with joy and I've never been so happy. I promise to love you with everything I have and to spend the rest of my life by your side."

Next came the lighting of the unity candle and Tom and Callie gave a beautiful white rose to both Jane and Pat.

With a few passages read by the minister, the ceremony came to a close. "Tom, you may kiss your bride."

Tom kissed Callie to the applause of the guests.

"Tom and Callie invite everyone to join them in the community room downstairs," the minister said.

The photographer asked Tom and Callie, Anna, Derek, Sophia, Jane and Pat to stay behind for pictures.

"I can't believe you pulled all this together so fast," Callie said.

"Well, not exactly fast. Truth be told, I started planning this when we came back from Thanksgiving weekend," he said.

"You did?"

"Yes. Everyone pitched in."

"I can't believe all of you kept it a secret."

"I almost blurted it out a couple of times," Tom said with a chuckle. "It's been the longest month of my life."

The reception, with all the Sullivan brothers as well as most of the townspeople, was everything that Callie could have hoped for. Everyone had a good time and the hours flew by with good food, toasts and plenty of dancing.

"Are you ready to leave, Mrs. Sullivan?" Tom asked as he twirled her on the dance floor.

Callie nodded. "I thought you'd never ask."

"Let's say goodbye to Sophia and then we can leave." They spotted Sophia sitting with Jane and walked to their table. "Sophia," Tom said.

The little girl ran to him. "Daddy!"

"Sweetie, Miss Callie and I are leaving now. You're going to stay with Nana, okay?"

The little girl nodded. "Okay. Then Miss Callie will be my Mommy?"

"Yes, Sweetie. Miss Callie is your new Mommy." Tom and then Callie kissed her. "Bye, Sophia. I'll see you soon," Callie said.

They said their goodbyes to the rest of the group and headed to the Bradbury Country Inn for their wedding night. It was a short drive to the Inn, and before long, Tom was inserting the keycard into the slot of the bridal suite. He pushed open the door, scooped Callie up in his arms, and carried her over the threshold.

Callie threw her head back and laughed. "Such a gentleman. I love you."

Tom kissed her. "I love you, too."

The fireplace had a welcoming fire lit, and there was a bottle of champagne and a dish of strawberries on the small table. He set her down on the chair. "Care for some champagne?"

"I would love some."

Tom poured them both a glass. "Here's to my beautiful bride," he said, clinking their glasses together.

"To my wonderful husband," she said.

"I hope you're happy," Tom said.

"I've never been happier. I can't believe everything you did to make our wedding so perfect."

"Well, I have one more surprise for you," he said, reaching for a long cardboard tube next to the table.

"Oh, Tom. What now? You've already done so much."

Tom opened the tube and pulled out an architectural drawing. He unrolled it on the bed. "I wanted to give you the perfect wedding present."

Callie looked at the drawing and tears welled in her eyes. It was her dream home—a Craftsman-style home with a wide porch in the front. "How did you know?"

"Do you like it?"

"I love it. It's everything I ever dreamed of in a home."

"Good. Anna told me about the home you lost. I want us to start our life in a home that is only ours."

Callie was crying freely now.

"Hey, I didn't mean to make you cry," Tom said, pulling her into his arms.

"I'm just so happy," Callie said in between sobs.

Tom held her until her tears stopped. "My darling, you mean everything to me. There isn't anything I wouldn't do for you, including designing your dream home. It will be a home full of love for our children."

"Our children?"

"Of course, as many as you'd like. I'm sure Sophia would love to have a little brother or sister," he said, caressing her cheek.

Callie stood on tiptoe and kissed her husband. "Make love to me, Tom."

Tom unzipped her dress and the chiffon creation floated to the floor. "You're so beautiful." He picked her up and gently laid her down on the bed. He shrugged out of his clothes and lay next to her. His fingers traced her curves as he kissed her deeply.

Callie's hands explored her husband's body. Desire surged through her and she pressed against him, inviting him to know her. Their lovemaking took her to heights she'd never known before.

When their appetite was sated, she lay nestled in her husband's arms. "That was incredible," she said in a sleepy voice. "This day has been like a dream—every girl's perfect fairy tale with the handsome prince."

Tom chuckled. "My darling Callie. You deserved this and more."

Callie leaned up on her elbow, looking down at her husband's face. "To think, a snap decision brought me to Bradbury. I was running away from a bad situation and never expected to meet anyone here. I had no idea what to expect. I just knew I needed a change. It was the best decision of my life because it brought me to you."

Tom caressed her cheek. "Thank goodness for snap decisions."

Callie brushed her lips against his.

"My dear sweet Mrs. Sullivan," he said as he pulled her to him and they began another wonderful journey together.

THE END

DEBRA ELIZABETH

SECOND CHANCE Christmas

Chapter 1

THE ELEVATOR DOORS SWOOSHED OPEN and Megan Duffy stepped out into the dark lobby. No one was here at this early hour and she relished the quiet time before the law firm began to buzz with activity. She was smartly dressed in a white silk blouse and navy pencil skirt, and her blonde hair was pulled back in a bun at the nape of her neck. Her heels echoed on the marble floor as she walked by the wall of glass windows and doors belonging to the partners' offices. Glancing through the outside windows, she took in the high-rise buildings that dominated the landscape. The building housing the firm of Grayson, Wexler and Manning was in the center of the corporate hubbub and she loved every minute of it.

She had wanted to be a lawyer for as long as she could remember. Her interest in the law had sparked early in her teenage years, when plans for a super highway project in her local community were approved. It would wipe out virtually all the woods on either side of it. The highway was only a mile from her home. Although she rallied support in the neighborhood against the project, in the end, the super highway was built and it broke her heart to see those bulldozers raze everything in their path. That's when she knew she wanted to be a lawyer and make a difference. She wanted to fight for the little guys and make a difference.

John Grayson had hired her immediately after she passed the bar, and she had been practicing at the firm for the past eight years. The long hours she put in had certainly honed her skills. Her specialty was environmental law and she was the most passionate about saving wildlife habitat whenever she could. Every victory counted, whether it is a large moneymaking case or a pro-bono one. They were all important in her estimation.

The sky was beginning to brighten and the spectacular view of the city from the twenty-seventh floor spread out before her. It was a cool morning, but ninety-degree heat and humidity was forecasted for later today. It was only May and if it was this hot so early in the season, she didn't want to think about what the summer temperatures would bring. The uncomfortable temperatures didn't matter to her though, because today she'd be in the office all day going over briefs.

She rounded the corner and spotted a light on in the conference room further down the hall. "Who's here so early?" she murmured. She hurried along the corridor, and stopped short when she looked inside. She would know his profile anywhere—strong jawline, perfect nose, full lips and broad shoulders. Her heart skipped a beat at the sight of him sitting at the conference table. His dark brown hair had recently been trimmed, and when he turned at her approach, a smile lit up her face. Jason Beckman, her boyfriend for the past two years, rose from his chair and she rushed into his strong arms.

"I missed you so much, my darling," she said in between kisses. "Why didn't you call me? I would have picked you up at the airport."

"I wanted to surprise you."

"You certainly did that. I wasn't expecting you until next week."

He arched an eyebrow. "Shall I leave and come back then?" he asked in a teasing tone.

Megan playfully slapped his arm. "Don't you dare! I hate these long trips you go on. I miss you so much. The apartment is empty without you."

"I miss you too, Megs." Jason took her hand. "Come and sit for a minute. I want to talk to you about something."

Megan dutifully sat in the chair, not quite sure what Jason had up his sleeve. It was unusual for him to want a sit-down discussion. He was more the spontaneous type. "What is it?"

Instead of sitting in the chair beside her, he bent down on one knee and pulled a small blue box out of his pocket. Her breath caught and butterflies fluttered in her chest. He was going to propose. She'd had no idea he was entertaining that idea, although it was the path she had hoped they were moving toward. They had gotten especially close in the past few months, and she knew Jason was the guy for her. He was driven, hardworking, and their passion in the bedroom made her tingle from head to toe. Their life together was perfect and she'd never been happier.

He opened the box to reveal a beautiful three-carat emerald-cut diamond that sparkled in the light. "Megan Duffy, will you marry me?"

Megan opened her mouth to speak, but no words came out. She was so overwhelmed with emotion that she barely managed to bob her head 'yes' before tears of joy streamed down her cheeks.

Jason pulled the ring out of the box and slid it on the third finger of her left hand. "There. It looks perfect, like it was meant for you."

She threw her arms around his neck and kissed him long and deep. Her heart swelled with love for this man. This was the best surprise he'd ever given her. When they finally broke apart, she slumped back in the chair and held up her hand to admire the ring. "I love you so much. It's the most beautiful ring I've ever seen. How did you know I liked emerald cut stones? I've never mentioned it."

He gave her a slow and sexy smile, revealing straight white teeth. "It suited you the best. As soon as I saw it, I knew it was perfect," he said, sitting in the chair next to her.

When she woke up this morning, she had no idea that it was going to be the happiest day of her life. Jason wanted her—Mr. Perfect, with his incredible body, sky blue eyes that burned holes through her and that dazzling smile which brought out his dimples, wanted her, Megan Duffy. She was floating on cloud nine with joy.

Megan wiped the tears from her cheeks. "I'm stunned. I had no idea you were thinking about getting married."

Jason leaned forward and kissed her again. He pushed a strand of hair that had escaped its pins behind her ear and lovingly caressed her cheek. "Are you ready for your next surprise?" he asked, as he took her hands in his.

She inhaled sharply. "Another one?" She didn't think the day could get any better and eagerly waited to hear what Jason had in store for her next.

"It's why I came back early. I couldn't wait to tell you."

Megan sat up straighter. "Tell me what?" A sudden uneasy feeling rose in her throat, but she pushed it away. She was overreacting. Nothing was going to spoil this day.

"I've worked here for ten years and I love this firm, but I got a better offer."

"Really? What's better than a partnership here?"

"A Senior Partnership."

Her mouth fell open. "Wow, that's fantastic. I didn't know they were entertaining the thought of another senior partner."

"Not here, Megs. At Chung & Chung, but soon to be Chung, Chung and Beckman."

Megan stared at Jason, trying hard to comprehend what he was saying to her. She'd heard of that firm before, but couldn't quite place it. It took a few moments before it dawned on her. "But, aren't they in Hong Kong?"

"Exactly. I met the partners six months ago and we started talking. They were very persistent in trying to recruit me. It took some time, but they finally offered me what I wanted."

She pulled her hands free. "Six months ago? You've been talking about this for months with them and you didn't think to tell me? Why would you keep something so important a secret from me?"

Jason reached for her hand again, but Megan pulled back. "I didn't want to say anything until it was a done deal and believe me, it's a fantastic deal. I'll be overseeing the Banking and Finance Division and you'll be in Commercial Law."

"Wait. What do you mean I'll be in Commercial Law? Did you negotiate a partnership for me too?"

For the first time since he started talking, he looked away, rubbing the dark stubble on his chin. Megan knew that wasn't a good sign. Jason had always been straightforward with her and never shied away from confrontations.

"Not exactly. It's an associate position, but—"

She didn't let him finish. "Are you kidding? An associate position? Why would I accept a lowly associate position when I've just made partner here?"

He stood and began to pace before turning around to face her. "Because it's a good deal."

"A good deal?" she asked, her voice rising with indignation. "For you, maybe, but not for me. I've slaved for this firm, working nights and weekends, and it took me eight years to make partner. What made you think I'd give that up? You're not making any sense."

Jason took a seat and grasped her hand, giving it a gentle squeeze. "To be with me. Don't you see? It's a once in a lifetime opportunity and I even signed a provisional agreement for the sale and purchase on a fantastic place before I left Hong Kong. You'll love it. It's perfect for us."

Megan's head was spinning. It was all too much. Not only did Jason not respect her hard work in making partner at Grayson, Wexler and Manning, but he also had gone ahead and bought a home without even consulting her. As she sat there staring at the man she adored, her future life flashed before her eyes—day after day of boring corporate law in a foreign country with no friends or family around, watching Jason excel at the firm while she toiled away in the pit. She was his trophy wife and he expected her to play her part without any respect for her abilities.

Is that all he thought of her? A worthless trophy wife? How dare he? She would be no one's trophy wife, sitting meekly in the corner while the men talked. A slow burning anger swelled in her chest and her eyes flashed. She'd thought she knew everything there was to know about Jason, but now it seemed she didn't know him at all.

"No."

Jason let go of her hand and his brow furrowed. "No? What does that mean?"

Megan stood, took the diamond ring off her finger and placed it on the table. "I can't marry you. Nor will I move to Hong Kong and take an associate position. I thought you respected my ability as a lawyer, but also as your partner in life. I guess I was wrong on both counts. This deal you say is fantastic may be the perfect deal for you, but it's not for me. I won't be your trophy wife, following you halfway around the world. So my answer is no to everything."

"Megs, can we—"

She needed to get away from him. Their perfect moment had shattered and she felt those shards pierce her heart one by one. The pain of Jason's actions threatened to overwhelm her. How could she have been so wrong? She'd thought he was the man she'd spend the rest of her life with, have children with, grow old with, but that wasn't going to happen now. Tears welled in her eyes. This day had turned into a disaster before it had even started.

"I have to go," she said, grabbing her briefcase and running from the room. Down the corridor she flew, until she reached her office. She closed the window blinds overlooking her assistant's desk and locked the door before slumping into her chair. Hot tears spilled down her cheeks. They were the tears of a broken heart, in mourning for the life with Jason that she would never have now. Her perfect life was in shambles. Sobs wracked her thin frame and she buried her face in her hands. In a matter of minutes, she had gone from blissfully happy to the absolute depths of despair, and she didn't know how she would ever recover from it.

A knock on her door interrupted her sorrow. "Go away. I don't want to talk to you."

Jason knocked again. "Megs, come on. Can't we talk about this?"

Megan flew out of her chair and threw open the door. "Now you want to talk? It's a little late for that, isn't it? You've got our whole life planned and you never once bothered to consult me about it. Come to think of it, isn't that how it's always been? All those surprises you planned were just your way of getting exactly what you wanted, when you wanted it. You planned the restaurants we ate in, planned our vacation destinations, which apartment we rented; you planned everything down to the smallest detail. I was a fool not to have seen this before. You don't care about me. You just want someone who is appropriate on your arm—the dutiful wife who will do your bidding and make a good impression on your associates."

Jason narrowed his eyes. "Is that what you think?"

Megan swiped at the tears on her cheeks. "You know what really gets me? During this whole thing, you never once said you loved me, that I was the woman you couldn't live without. Not even once."

The muscles in his face tightened and she could see the steely resolve in his eyes. She'd hit a nerve and there was no going back now.

He squared his shoulders. "Fine. If that's the way you feel, then so be it. I'll have my things packed and out of the apartment by the end of the day. Have a good life, Megan." He turned and stormed off.

All the fight and indignation left her as she watched him walk down the hall and out of her life. Had she done the right thing, or had she just made the biggest mistake of her life?

Chapter 2

MEGAN COULDN'T CONCENTRATE ON THE brief sitting in front of her. She'd read the same paragraph three times and still didn't know what it said. She couldn't remember how long she had cried over Jason leaving her earlier that morning, but she had managed to go to the ladies room and redo her make-up before her assistant, Nancy, had arrived. She blamed her red eyes on allergies and no one questioned her.

Her computer pinged and she looked at the email sitting in her inbox. It was from the senior partners, calling for a partner meeting today at three p.m. She inwardly groaned. That was the last thing she needed today. She had a pretty good idea what the topic of conversation was going to be. She hoped to make a quick exit after the meeting to avoid the bevy of questions that would come her way once Jason's departure from the firm was announced. Their relationship was not a secret and it would be natural for people to ask if she would be joining him in Hong Kong. Her hurt was too raw to talk about their breakup and the last thing she wanted to do was cry at a partners' meeting. She would not let them see her weak. She had to hold it together.

Nancy knocked on her door before opening it. "Megan, five minutes."

"Thanks. I remembered."

Nancy nodded and returned to her desk.

At the appointed time, Megan walked into the conference room. Jason was sitting at one end of the table with the other senior partners. She took a seat by the door. Her heart was beating wildly, but she steeled herself. Her gaze became calm as she hid her emotions behind an invisible barrier. She was determined to hold her inner turmoil in check.

The room quickly filled, with many wondering aloud why a partners' meeting was being called on such short notice. It was highly unusual and caused a stir among her colleagues.

Jane Simonson, a partner specializing in corporate espionage, leaned toward her. She was in her mid-thirties and one of the smartest people Megan knew. She and Jane had had many an interesting conversation about corporate wheeling and dealing. Megan admired her and considered her a friend, but today she wasn't in a talkative mood, not even to Jane.

"Any idea what's going on today?" Jane asked.

Megan kept her face neutral. "Not a clue."

Before Jane could ask any more questions, John Grayson, the senior managing partner, called the meeting to order.

"Thank you all for coming. I know you're busy and this won't take long." John waited until he had every eye in the room riveted on him, then continued. "Jason Beckman has one of the brightest minds I've ever encountered and he has certainly made his mark here at the firm. Unfortunately, we're not the only ones who've noticed his abilities. Jason has been offered an excellent opportunity to make his mark in another part of the world. He'll be joining Chung and Chung of Hong Kong, soon to be Chung, Chung and Beckman."

The room exploded with congratulations. Megan kept her eyes on John as several heads swiveled between her and Jason, asking the unspoken question of whether she would be joining him. It took every ounce of her willpower not to run from the room.

When the room quieted, John continued. "I've talked with Jason about his pending cases and who will be taking on his clients and covering pending litigation. I'll need Tom, Jane, Bob and Susan to meet in my office today at five. We can go over everything in detail then." John turned to Jason. "Would like to say anything?"

Jason stood and buttoned his suit coat, looking every inch a senior partner. "I want to thank John for his unwavering support in guiding my career. I'm a better lawyer because of his guidance. I would also like to thank my colleagues. I've enjoyed my time here at Grayson,

Wexler and Manning. I'm more than a little sad to leave, but I'm very excited to forge a new path with Chung & Chung. Thank you."

Before Jane had a chance to grill her, Megan slipped out the door. She wasn't in the mood to explain to anyone what had happened earlier between her and Jason. The last thing she needed today was to see pity in her colleague's eyes. Everyone knew Jason was a star. She was sure that more than a few of the lawyers had thought they were mismatched as a couple, that he could do better than her—someone more established, more connected, and with the star power to match his. Well, that didn't matter anymore. The sooner Jason left for Hong Kong, the better off she would be. Except she wasn't going to feel better for a long time, whether he was here or not.

She walked back to her office in a daze. She felt so empty inside, like her heart had been ripped out of her chest and stomped on.

"Hey, are you okay?" Nancy asked as Megan walked by.

Megan brushed a strand of hair out of her face. "Yeah, why do you ask?"

"Because you look like you just lost your best friend?"

Nancy's genuine concern melted the last chink in Megan's armor. Her resolve cracked and fresh tears spilled down her cheeks.

Nancy jumped up from her chair and put her arm around Megan's shoulders. "Come on. Let's get in your office. Do you want to tell me what's going on?"

Megan slumped in her chair. "Jason proposed this morning."

Nancy closed the office door and took the seat in front of her desk. "He did?" She glanced at Megan's finger. "No ring?"

Megan grabbed a tissue and wiped her eyes. "Yes, there was a ring. A gorgeous emerald-cut ring."

"That sounds wonderful, but I don't understand. Why are you crying?"

It took long minutes between bouts of crying for Megan to tell Nancy the whole sordid tale. "I can't believe he thought so little of me and my accomplishments. He just expected me to drop everything and follow him halfway around the world."

Nancy, never one for coddling, spoke without sugarcoating the truth. "Well, men are jerks sometimes and Jason ranks right up at the top. I suppose it's better you found out now than after you married him. That would be so much worse, especially if you had moved to Hong Kong."

Megan nodded. "I know you're right, but right now, it hurts too much. I thought he was the one, you know? My Prince Charming, and I was going to live happily ever after."

Nancy snorted. "Ha! I've never met a man yet that lived up to that fantasy. I think it's an absolute impossibility. No one is that perfect."

Megan couldn't help but chuckle at that. "You're probably right."

"When is he leaving?"

"I honestly don't know. I assume it will be in the next few days, maybe a week at most. I'm sure the office will have a field day with this news, especially when I don't leave the firm to follow."

"Don't give it a second thought. I'll take care of any wagging tongues."

Megan stared at her assistant. Nancy was young and ambitious and a force to reckon with around the office. She reminded Megan a lot of her younger self right out of college. Nancy was smart and knew what she wanted. She was pursuing her own law degree at night. Megan had no doubt that she'd be a success in whatever field of law she chose to pursue. "Have I told you how much I appreciate everything you do for me?"

Nancy nodded. "All the time. Now why don't you get out of here for the rest of the day? Get some fresh air and clear your head. I'll reschedule your last meeting."

"Excellent suggestion as always," Megan said. She grabbed the briefs on her desk and stuffed them into her briefcase. "Thanks for the sympathetic ear."

"Anytime." Nancy stood and opened the door. "See you tomorrow."

"Yes, you will. Bye."

Chapter 3

FOR THE NEXT WEEK, MEGAN did her utmost best to avoid Jason. He had been true to his word and moved his belongings out of their apartment the same day as their breakup. He didn't take much, but his absence was felt every morning when she strolled into their walk-in closet. His side was bare. He'd even taken the coat hangers, although she shouldn't have been surprised about that. He was insistent that only a certain style of wooden hanger would do for his clothes. The more she thought about it, it was probably for the best. At least she wouldn't be reminded of him every time she pulled something from the closet.

Every day was the same—slog through the mountain of work on her desk, only to go home at night and cry herself to sleep in their big empty bed. How long would she feel like her heart was being squeezed? Some nights, she couldn't catch her breath. She tried to tell herself that it was for the best like Nancy had suggested, but she didn't feel like that now. She wanted to rush down to his office and throw herself into his arms one last time, but she knew it wouldn't change anything. She had unmasked and confronted him with his selfish ways. There was no going back to the way things had been between them. She and Jason were over. It was time to put him out of her head; that is, if only she knew how.

A knock on her door interrupted her thoughts, and when she looked up, she was surprised to see John Grayson standing in her doorway.

"Megan, do you have a minute?" he asked.

"Of course, please come in."

"Thanks. I won't take much of your time." John, the managing senior partner, was a tall stately man with silver-white hair and soft brown eyes. He was the one who had hired Megan and mentored her in the early days of her career. She would be forever grateful to him for his help and support.

"What can I do for you, John?"

He took a seat. "Listen, I know this week has been hard on you."

Megan inwardly groaned. The last thing she wanted was for John to be sympathetic about her breakup with Jason. She was trying to put him behind her, but it was difficult with colleagues coming in and expressing their condolences about her love life. She didn't want John to go down that path as well.

She tried to smile, but failed miserably. "Hasn't been the best, that's for sure."

John nodded. "I get it, I do. Jason is a star and I knew the day would come when he would leave the firm. His ambition has set him on a different path and I wish him well. I sincerely mean that."

Megan wrung her hands in her lap. She was trying to hold it together, but she needed John to come to the point, and fast, before she starting crying again. "That's true. Is there something I can do for you?"

John shook his head. "No, there's nothing. I wanted to come and express my gratitude that you're not going with him."

"What?"

"Look, losing Jason was a foregone conclusion. It was only a matter of when. We're not big enough for him. But you, on the other hand, are a different story."

Megan sat up straighter, intrigued by John's statement. "I am?"

"Yes, you are. Maybe I'm a little biased, but you're very important to this firm. You're smart, good in court, and you know the law inside and out. I'm glad I didn't have to counter an outside offer and put you in the untenable position of having to choose between a life with Jason or staying here."

Megan was shocked by what she was hearing. John would have made a counter proposal to keep her at the firm? She'd had no idea he valued her that much. "That's very kind of you to say, John. I'm sure Jason must have told you that I will not be joining him in Hong Kong."

"That's all he said, but I have a feeling it was much more complicated than that."

Megan nodded. "It was, but I won't bore you with the details. I want to thank you for your vote of confidence, though."

John stood. "No need to thank me. You've earned your partnership here and I hope you'll be happy to stay here for a good long while."

"Thank you, John. That's wonderful to hear. I appreciate you telling me that."

"My pleasure."

She watched the senior partner walk out of office before she slumped back in the chair. She smiled for the first time in a week. John's visit had done more to lift her spirits than any of her colleagues' kind words. She was valued here. It felt good to know that. With a renewed sense of energy, she got back to work.

Nancy poked her head into the office at the end of the day. "Megan, a bunch of us are going out for a drink. Want to join us?"

Megan shook her head. "No, I don't think so. I'm going to finish up this and then I'm going home to take a long hot soak in the bath."

"Are you sure? You can't hide away in your apartment forever, you know."

She chuckled. "I know and I appreciate your concern, but I'm opting for the bath tonight. Have a good time."

"Okay, see you tomorrow."

"Good night."

It was nearly eight p.m. when she finally shut her computer off. She grabbed her briefcase and headed down the corridor toward the elevators. A nice glass of wine and a hot soak sounded wonderful to her right about now. When she turned the corner, she was faced with exactly the situation she'd hope to avoid.

Jason was standing there and he turned at her approach. "Hi, Megs."

The sound of his voice nearly melted her. That same familiar tone that she had missed so much this week and had tried so hard to avoid. She was riveted in place and couldn't find her voice.

Jason walked toward her. "Are you all right?"

That snapped her out of her stupor. No, she was not all right. How could he think that? Unless, of course, he was fine about their breakup and was already moving on to his next conquest. "I'm fine. Thanks."

"Shall we share the elevator one last time? I'm leaving in the morning."

"No. I just remembered I left something in my office. Good luck with your new job," she said as she turned away.

He touched her arm. "Come on, Megs. Don't be like that. We can still be friends, can't we?"

She looked over her shoulder at his handsome smiling face. A wall of armor closed over her heart. "No, Jason. We cannot be friends." She walked away without a backward glance.

Chapter 4

THE BRISK WIND BLEW THROUGH her hair, sending a chill down her neck as Megan tugged opened the door to the office building. After a warm fall, the weather was turning bitterly cold with no transition days in between. One day it was fifty degrees and the next day it was seventeen. Ridiculous weather, as far as she was concerned.

She shivered as she walked through the lobby to the bank of elevators.

"Morning, Megan," the guard on duty called to her.

"Hey, Bill. How's it going?"

Bill shrugged. "Same thing, different day, except it's a lot colder."

Megan chuckled. "I hear you. Not a fan of this cold. Have a good one, Bill."

"You too."

The elevator door opened and she stepped inside. It quickly climbed to the twenty-seventh floor. It had been six months since Jason had left her and she was finally finding her center—no more of that crushing weight on her chest cutting off her breath or that searing pain in her heart that threatened to overwhelm her at the mention of his name. She'd gone through the other side of her grief and the world was a happy place once more. Well, maybe not happy as much as she could get through a day without tears. That was a step in the right direction as far as she was concerned.

Her professional life had gotten a shot in the arm as well. She had won a hard-fought appeal battle in a class action suit against an oil company for destroying a hefty chunk of coastline when one of its tankers ran aground. It would bring in millions for the firm, but more than that, it had given her an infusion of confidence and self-esteem. She was a good lawyer and John Grayson's accolades over the win felt well deserved. She had almost forgotten Jason's lack of respect for her abilities.

Almost.

She wondered if she would ever get over the sting of him devaluing her. Megan chided herself. It didn't matter what Jason thought anymore. This victory went a long way in soothing away that hurt. As she made her way to her office, she was surprised to see Nancy typing away on her laptop.

"Hey, good morning," Megan said. "You're here early."

Nancy looked up. "I could say the same for you."

"Oh, I'm always here early. I like the quiet before all the busy bees get here."

Nancy chuckled. "Would one of those busy bees be me?"

Megan felt herself flush. She hadn't meant any insult. "No, I didn't mean it that way. I just meant it's quiet here before everyone gets in, that's all."

Nancy raised an eyebrow. "Megan, chill. I knew what you meant."

"Good. So, why are here?"

"I needed to look up something in the library, and while I was here, I figured I would get this paper written. It's due tomorrow and I didn't want to burn the midnight oil getting it done."

"Sounds like a plan to me. I'll just ignore you for the next ninety minutes. How's that?"

"Perfect. Thank you."

"No problem," Megan said, walking into her office. She turned on her computer and waited for her daily calendar application to come up. She needed to see if Nancy had scheduled any major meetings for her over the next two weeks.

As luck would have it, no major client meetings had been scheduled for the rest of December. She put a note 'no more meetings' in the banner, alerting Nancy to her plans to take a few days off. She planned to catch up with John Grayson later in the day to make sure he didn't need her for anything before she took off and headed to her family's cabin retreat up north in the woods. She hadn't been to the cabin in almost two years and it seemed like the perfect spot to relax and renew her soul.

She loved the quiet of the woods and had even taken Jason there once, but he began chomping at the bit as soon as he learned there was no internet connection up there. Their romantic interlude had lasted only one day before they were heading back to the city. It was one more instance where Jason had ruled her life. Now that she was out of the relationship, she could see it for what it was, and realized their marriage wouldn't have lasted. Sooner or later, she'd have rebelled against his controlling ways. Nancy was right. It was better to find that out now.

Three days later, on December twenty-first, she was driving up the coast, enjoying the scenery while listening to the sound of the waves crashing against the rocks. It wasn't the quickest route to take to the cabin, but she didn't care. The scenery was breathtaking and she had no timetable to keep for the next two weeks. The weather had warmed a bit, but certainly not enough to put the top down on her BMW Z4 roadster—which she referred to as 'The Red Bullet.' The car was an absolute indulgence and her one extravagance in life. She loved this car. Its only drawback was the lack of luggage space. It wasn't an issue in the city, but it was challenging to take on a long trip. Her suitcase took up all the room in the trunk and groceries lined the passenger floor and seat.

She would have to go to the local general store to pick up whatever else she needed. She hoped that old Jake was still there. He was a fixture in the little town of Adin-Lookout. The town was small and Jake knew everyone. He was usually right on the mark when it came to figuring out folks. Jake hadn't said much when he met Jason, but she could tell by the grim set of his mouth that he didn't like him much. Megan was looking forward to seeing him again and telling him he had been right about Jason.

It was late afternoon when she finally pulled into town. She parked the car and ambled into the general store. There were a few customers ahead of her, but she didn't recognize any of them. She wondered if they found the quiet life in Adin-Lookout a great alternative to the hustle and bustle of the city. She was certainly looking forward to the respite and vowed not to let so much time go by before she came up for another visit. While she waited for her turn at the counter, she puttered around the store, picking up a few items that she had forgotten to pack. She also grabbed some pancake mix. She hadn't made pancakes in forever and just holding the box made her mouth water. She sauntered down the aisle to the refrigerated case and grabbed a pound of butter and a container of Half & Half for her morning coffee.

"Did you find everything you need?" a husky voice behind her asked.

Megan turned around and came face-to-face with a well-toned chest. Her gaze traveled up past the chiseled jawline, full kissable lips to land on intense green eyes. Black hair curling around his ears and brushing the top of his shirt collar completed the picture for Mr. Sexy. Her mouth fell open. "Uh, yeah. Thanks," she managed to spit out. This guy oozed sex appeal in a rugged sort of way. The beginning of a five o'clock shadow added to the attraction and it certainly didn't hurt that he filled out his flannel shirt and blue jeans to perfection.

"Snap out of it," her inner voice scolded. *"Full kissable lips? What's wrong with you? It's not like you've never seen a sexy guy before."*

"Here, let me help you with some of this," he said.

"Would you mind grabbing the pancake mix before I drop it?"

"Sure thing," he said with ready smile of perfect white teeth.

Megan followed him back to the front of the store and put her items on the counter. "I'll also need some bundles of wood."

"Okay. If you pull your truck around, I'll load them up for you."

"Um, I don't have a truck. Jake always offered to deliver the wood for me." She looked around. "By the way, where is Jake?"

"He's probably sitting by the fire enjoying a cold beer, if I know Jake."

"Oh, I thought he'd be here," Megan said, trying to avoid gawking at the gorgeous stranger.

"No, he retired last year. I own the store now. I'm Ryker McCabe," he said, extending his hand.

Megan felt a shiver race up her spine when their hands met in a firm handshake. "Wow, I never thought Jake would retire. He's been here for as long as I can remember."

"Guess he thought it was time. So, how many bundles of wood do you need and where should I deliver them?"

"Sorry, where are my manners? I'm Megan Duffy and my family's cabin is a few miles out of town at the top of the hill on Old Mill Road. How about three bundles to start?"

"I'm sure I can find it," Ryker said. "Let me ring you up and then I'll see about the wood."

Megan hesitated. She didn't want to seem too forward, but she needed that wood tonight unless she wanted to sleep in cold storage. "Why don't I take some wood with me to get a fire started? The cabin will be cold and I don't want to impose on your generosity to bring the rest up to me."

Ryker flashed her a sexy grin that highlighted his dimples. "It's no problem. I can follow you if you'd like. It's almost closing time."

Megan hesitated. "Are you sure?"

"No problem. That will be $57.35 including the wood."

She hadn't even noticed him packing up her groceries. She'd been too busy staring at him and drinking in his features, especially his eyes. She'd never seen eyes that green before. *Stop it!* her inner voice screamed. She was acting like a schoolgirl and a blush rose up her neck and painted her cheeks pink. "What's the delivery charge? I'm happy to pay that now too." She reached into her wallet and pulled out three twenty-dollar bills.

She saw Ryker's eyes roam her body. "No charge for you, Megan Duffy," he said in a satiny-smooth voice as he handed her the change.

She put the change in her wallet.

"I'll be with you in a minute," he said, while pulling the cash from the register and stuffing it in a night deposit bag.

Megan reached for the bag of groceries. "Thanks. I'll meet you outside. I'm in the red BMW."

"Okay." He walked behind her, and when she went outside, he locked the door and flipped over the sign. "CLOSED" now greeted any potential customers.

Megan opened the passenger side door and rearranged her packages so the bag of groceries would fit, got behind the wheel, and waited for Ryker to appear. She didn't have to wait long. He pulled up behind her in a silver Ram pick-up truck. When she looked in her rear view mirror, all she saw was truck grill. Her little sports car was definitely out of its element up here in the woods.

She gave him a wave, stepped on the gas, and drove out of town.

It didn't take long to reach the cabin. The smell of pine greeted her when she got out of the car and walked to the front door. She fumbled for the key in her purse, very much aware that Ryker was standing behind her with a bundle of wood. "Sorry, I should have pulled the key out sooner."

"Don't worry about. I'm not in any hurry."

She turned the key in the lock and pushed open the door. Dust floated in the air from the whoosh of cold air. The furniture was covered with white sheets and it was evident that no one had been here in a while.

"Don't come up here much, huh?" Ryker said, striding over to the fireplace.

"No, not much in the last two years. My brother was transferred to the East Coast last year, so the cabin is hardly getting any use at all these days."

"That's too bad. It's a great place."

"Well, I plan to use it more often now," she said, before going outside and gathering more bags to carry in.

Ryker followed her. "Here, let me help you with those," he said, grabbing some of the bundles out of the car.

"Thanks."

Megan clicked open the trunk and grabbed her suitcase. After putting the suitcase in the bedroom, she walked back to the kitchen to begin unloading the grocery bags.

Ryker rubbed his hands together. "It's cold in here. Let me get the fire going."

"Thank you. I appreciate your help."

With plenty of kindling wood stacked beside the fireplace, Ryker had no trouble lighting the wood. The fire was soon blazing and sending much needed warmth into the main room. "Oh, that feels great," Megan called out from the kitchen.

Ryker strode over to her. "Anything else I can help you with?"

A warm feeling enveloped her as she stared at him. She felt a tiny crack open in the armor around her tender heart.

How about a long slow kiss that curls my toes?

Chapter 5

Ryker couldn't help but stare at the delicate beauty standing before him. Her reddish gold hair framed the face of an angel. An angel with beautiful blue eyes and a sprinkle of freckles across her nose that only added to her allure. He'd seen dozens of beautiful women in his travels, but none of them could hold a candle to Megan Duffy. There was something about her, though, a sadness that seemed to envelop her. Her vulnerability scored his heart. He wanted to wrap her in his arms and protect her against the world, or at the very least, spend more time with her. Would she understand that his offer of help was his way of telling her he wanted to be in her company without being too pushy about it? The last thing he wanted was to be too aggressive and scare her away.

Megan glanced up from the bag of groceries she was emptying. "Um...I really don't want to impose. I appreciate you driving up here with me to deliver the wood. I would have had to make a lot of trips in my car." She chuckled at the image of wood piled high in her sports car.

"It's no imposition at all. Glad to help out," he said.

Megan hesitated for only a moment. "Well, in that case, would you like to stay for dinner?"

Ryker smiled. "Yes. That would be great."

Megan pulled the last item out of the bag. "You might want to reconsider. All I have at the moment is pancake mix."

"I love pancakes," Ryker said with a chuckle.

And then she smiled at him. It was the most perfect smile he'd ever seen and his heart soared with joy. He didn't know why this young woman had such an effect on him, but he didn't care. He was going to savor it and hopefully nurture it into something more. Perhaps it was fate bringing them together at this exact moment, when all of the stars were in perfect alignment. Whatever it was, he was going to enjoy it.

"Oh, and I brought blueberries with me too. Shall I add those?"

"Sure. I'll go and stack the rest of the wood for you. Do you want it all in the house or on the porch?"

"By the hearth would be good. Thank you."

Ryker nodded and went outside to his truck. He pulled the last two bundles from the truck bed and began stacking them inside. Megan was puttering in the kitchen, humming to herself. He thought it was a good sign.

People who were humming were usually happy. Could he dare to hope her good mood was in part because of him? That would certainly make his day complete. By the time he'd stacked all the wood and stripped off the furniture covers, dinner was ready.

"Shall we eat on the couch by the fire?" she asked. "It's still a little chilly in here."

Ryker looked at the stack of pancakes on his plate. "You feeding an army here?"

Megan grabbed the maple syrup. "Yeah, sorry about that. I made more batter than I thought. Don't feel you have to eat them all. Want maple syrup?"

He nodded and she poured a generous amount over the stack. "Thanks. They smell good."

"I made coffee too. Want some?"

"Sure, but let me get it. You go sit. How do you like your coffee?"

"Two sugars and a splash of Half & Half," she said, picking up the plates and strolling into the living room.

Ryker pulled open a couple of cupboard doors before he found the coffee mugs. He took his black and made Megan's to her specifications. "Here you go," he said, setting the mug down on the table beside her.

"Thank you."

He took a seat beside her. Her closeness stirred a passion in him that he had thought was long buried. Being with her seemed so natural, as if they were meant to be together. He glanced sideways at her. She was busy diving into her stack of pancakes. He grabbed his fork and followed suit. "These are delicious," he said in between mouthfuls.

Megan cocked an eyebrow. "Did you expect any less?" she asked with a chuckle.

He had a mouthful of pancakes and no snappy comeback, so he just shook his head. They spent the next few minutes happily munching away. "So, how long do you plan to be up here?" he asked.

"Probably until after the holiday," Megan said. "I needed to get away from the city and couldn't think of a more peaceful place. I forgot how beautiful it was up here."

Ryker figured now was a good time to find out if she had a boyfriend. She wasn't wearing a ring, but that didn't always matter. Time to dive in and take a chance. "So, is your boyfriend joining you on Friday for Christmas?"

Megan paused with her fork halfway to her mouth. A look of sadness flitted across her face. "No. No boyfriend. Not exactly the Christmas I had envisioned this year, but it doesn't matter anymore."

"I'm sorry. I didn't mean to pry," Ryker said. Now he knew why she seemed so sad. She must have been hurt badly and he wished he could take the hurt away.

Megan put her hand on his forearm. "It's okay. We broke up last May. I'm over him now. How about you? What are your plans for Christmas?"

Ryker took a sip of coffee. "Kind of quiet too. I usually check on a few older folks in town. Mrs. Bracken loves this particular marmalade and I order it special for her. She's always so delighted when I bring it to her. Her husband died two years ago and she's alone now, so I make a point of visiting her when I can."

"That's really sweet of you," Megan said, giving his arm a squeeze.

"It's no bother. Just my way of giving back to the community, you know?"

Megan put her empty plate on the coffee table. She grabbed her mug of coffee and scooted back on the couch and hugged her knees to her chest. "Don't you love watching the fire crackle? I find it mesmerizing. I don't have a fireplace at my apartment in the city, so this is such a treat."

I find you mesmerizing and could watch you forever.

He was torn. He felt an overwhelming urge to kiss her, but was afraid she would push him away. Was it too soon? The last thing he wanted was to ruin their first evening together. "You're so beautiful," he said, reaching over and tucking a lock of her hair behind her ear. "I'm glad you decided to come up to the cabin."

She turned from the fire and looked at him. "Oh... thank you."

"No need to thank me. I only speak the truth."

He saw her look down and fumble with the hem of her sweater. Maybe he shouldn't have said that, but it just popped out. He didn't want to make her uncomfortable, so he did the next best thing. He set the mug down on the coffee table and stood. "I should get going. You must be tired."

Megan stood. "Thank you again for helping me."

"Not a problem."

"Next time, I'll cook you a proper dinner—a nice juicy steak. How's that?"

Ryker grinned from ear-to-ear. So, there would be a next time. "Perfect," he said as he walked to the door. With one more backward glance at her, he opened the door and headed out into the cool night air. She wanted to see him again. His sweet angel wanted to see him. It was a start. He began to whistle a lively tune as he drove down the mountain road back to town.

Chapter 6

MEGAN GATHERED UP THE DISHES and carried them to the sink. So many thoughts whirled around her mind.

What was I thinking telling Ryker I'd cook for him again?

Wasn't the reason I came up to the cabin in the first place to clear my head and put everything that happened with Jason finally behind me?

How can I get involved with Ryker when I'm not one hundred percent sure I'm over Jason?

Jason.

The memory of their breakup still stung, but surprisingly, that empty heartache didn't threaten to overwhelm her any more. Was the old adage, 'time heals all,' true? Or did the thought of spending time with hunky Ryker help those bad memories fade away?

Ryker.

She wasn't usually attracted to the outdoorsy type, but something about him captivated her. He was honest and caring, not like the pretentious lawyers she was used to interacting with. How many people did she know who would visit the elderly on Christmas? Of course, the answer was only one, and she had spent a lovely evening with him. His openness and lively banter had made her laugh and she'd found herself relaxing for the first time in months. It could have been the peacefulness of the cabin that made her smile, but then again, maybe it was Mr. Ryker McCabe who had brought that simple pleasure back into her life.

She finished cleaning up the kitchen and headed back to the couch. She put a few more logs on the fire and put the screen in place to keep the sparks from flying into room. She snuggled back into the couch cushions and pulled the fleece blanket around her.

Maybe it was time to stop living in the past and begin living in the present, especially if the present included seeing Ryker again.

THE NEXT MORNING, MEGAN took her time getting dressed, paying special attention to her hair and makeup. She was going into town to see Ryker and she wanted to look her best. She'd forgotten to get his cell phone number last night, or maybe she did that on purpose. She wasn't sure, but the one thing she was sure of was that little slip was the perfect excuse to see him again. She had offered to cook him a proper dinner and wanted to find out what night he was free. She slipped on a pair of black skinny jeans and a pale blue sweater. She knew the color would highlight the color of her eyes nicely and hoped Ryker would notice.

She pulled on her winter coat and headed out. There was a definite bite in the air as she walked to her car. She inhaled deeply, pulling the clean air into her lungs. She felt invigorated this morning, ready to take on the world. Or at least to talk with Ryker again without sounding like a complete idiot. She felt tongue-tied around him, especially when he looked at her with those amazing green eyes. It was almost as if he saw straight through to her soul, understood her with all her flaws, and still found her desirable. She hadn't felt desirable in a long time and although she wasn't looking to date anyone, Ryker's attention was flattering.

The ride into town didn't take long. While she drove around looking for a parking space, she noticed a few things had changed since the last time she was here. *Mary's Diner* was still there, but there was a new coffee shop on the opposite side of the street. Next to it was a used bookstore. She planned to peruse the bookstore before she left town and might even stop into the coffee shop, but right now, she wanted nothing more than to see Ryker. She found a parking space not far from the general store.

She took a deep breath, got out of the car and walked to the store. The doorbells chimed as Megan entered. There were quite a few customers shopping today and she had to wait her turn to speak to Ryker. While she waited, she walked to the refrigerated meat case to see what her options were for steak. She was surprised to find a good selection, including filet mignon, her favorite cut of beef. She selected two packages and headed over to the potato bin, where she picked out two large Idaho potatoes. The season was over for fresh vegetables, so she opted for a pre-packaged spring mix of lettuce. Rounding out her purchases, she picked up the milk and flour she would need to make homemade dinner rolls. Just looking at the items in her arms made her mouth water. It had been a long time since she cooked a homemade meal and even longer since she cooked it for someone else. Jason had always preferred to eat out.

By the time she walked to the front counter, Ryker was chatting with the last customer in line.

"Have a good day, Mrs. Bracken," he said to the older woman. "Are you sure you don't need help with that bag?"

Mrs. Bracken picked up the bag and shook her head. "Thank you, Ryker. I've got it. See you on Friday."

"Looking forward to it," he said to her receding back.

"Hi," Megan said, putting her items on the counter. "Guess there won't be any surprises about what I'm serving you for dinner, huh? The only question left is what night are you free?"

A smile split Ryker's face. "Hi, yourself. I'm glad to see you and I'm free any night you want."

"Good. How about tonight? My mouth is watering just looking at this meat."

"Happy to oblige. Tonight it is. I usually close up the store at six. How about seven?"

"Seven is perfect."

Megan watched his muscles ripple under his shirt as he bagged up the groceries. She imagined running her hands up his arms and over his chest, but most of all, she imagined what it would feel like to kiss his lips.

"Megan?"

Megan gave her head a little shake. She had to stop daydreaming about him, especially when he was standing in front of her. "I'm sorry. Was just thinking about... ummm...a work problem, that's all."

"No problem. I get it. Hard to leave the office at the office."

"Yeah, something like that," she said, twirling a lock of hair around her finger. "Well, I should go. I see that you've got more customers." She handed him the money and a shiver ran up her spine when their hands met.

"Such soft hands," Ryker said, tracing a line across her palm.

His touch had such an effect on her that it made her a little dizzy. She had a hard time thinking straight and wanted nothing more than for him to reach across the counter and kiss her.

"Thank you," she said, giving him her prettiest smile. "I should go. I have a few more errands to run. I'll see you later," she said, scooping up the bag.

"I'm looking forward to it," Ryker said.

Megan walked out into the sunshine, inwardly scolding herself.

Are you kidding? All of a sudden you're tongue-tied and daydreaming about kissing him again? Not that there's anything wrong with that, but daydreaming about him when he's right in front of you is weird.

Besides, you're only going to be around for a few days, a week at most, before you head back to the city. Don't start something you can't finish.

Her logical side said it would be foolish to start a new relationship, but for all the reasons she came up with why this was a bad idea, she kept coming back to the undeniable attraction she felt for him.

What was wrong with having a nice romantic dinner anyway?

Chapter 7

RYKER EXHALED WHEN MEGAN LEFT. She looked even more beautiful today than when he first laid eyes on her, if that was even possible. The sight of her made his heart thump loudly in his chest and he wondered if she could hear it. It was so unlike his usual reserved personality to act like a lovesick schoolboy, but all he had wanted to do was pull her into his arms and kiss her long and slow and deep. He'd almost done that very thing last night, but thought it might scare her off.

He hadn't known when she was going to come back into town and he'd forgotten to get her cell phone number last night. Thank goodness she came in today so he didn't make a fool of himself by showing up on her doorstep unannounced.

"Ryker?"

His attention shifted to the customer at the counter. "Hey, Phil. How's it going?" he asked the local lumberjack.

"Not bad. Heading up to the site now."

"How are Janice and the kids?"

Phil chuckled. "The house is a zoo now that all three of them are home on vacation."

"I bet. Christmas must be wild at your house."

"You know it is. With three kids under seven, there's not a quiet moment all day. But I wouldn't change it for the world," Phil said, handing Ryker money to pay for his coffee and bagel.

"Want a bag?"

"No, I'm good," he said, taking a bite out of the bagel as he turned to leave.

"Have a good one and be safe out there," Ryker called after him.

Ryker glanced at his watch—only ten-thirty in the morning. He wasn't seeing Megan until seven tonight. It was going to be a long day. Might as well get as much work done as he could and it would keep his mind occupied. He walked to the stockroom at the back of the store and began pulling boxes out. He needed to replenish a number of items on the selling floor. Sales were brisk this week leading up to Christmas, especially the baking items like flour and sugar. He'd been through the Christmas season before and made sure to order extra of both for this week.

The hours seemed to crawl by, but finally it was time to close the store. He locked the front door, flipped over the sign so "CLOSED" faced the street, and grabbed the cash from the register. He'd make a night deposit on his way home. Pulling on his jacket, he shut off the lights and went out the back door.

Forty-five minutes later, after a quick shower and a change of clothes, he was driving to Megan's cabin. He couldn't wait to see her again. Anxious thoughts rolled around in his head. Should I kiss her tonight? Would she welcome it? It would all depend on what signals she was giving off. He hoped that she was as into him as he was into her. To kiss those sweet lips would be like heaven on earth.

The miles sped by and soon he was pulling into the cabin's driveway. He took a deep breath and grabbed the bottles of wine he'd picked up along the way. He knocked on the front door, and when she opened the door, his heart seized. She was a vision dressed in a white sweater and gray slacks. Her honey blonde hair cascaded down her back and all he could think about was how wonderful it would feel to bury his hands in her curls. "Hi," was the only word he could get out.

"Hi. Come on in. It's freezing out there," she said, stepping back to allow him inside.

"Thanks. I wasn't sure what type of wine you preferred, so I brought a white and a red."

"Thank you. That's great. I actually prefer white. Never did develop a taste for red."

Ryker walked into the kitchen and took the wine out of the bag. "Can I pour you a glass?"

Megan followed him and pulled two wine glasses out of the cabinet. "Yes. I would love one."

He poured the wine and handed her a glass. "Thanks for inviting me for dinner," he said, clinking their glasses together.

"It's my pleasure," she said as she sipped the wine. "Oh, this is good."

Ryker's heart rate increased. She was beautiful, and for the moment, only had eyes for him. He wished he could save this moment forever. It was perfect. She was perfect. "Glad you like it." He glanced over to the dining table. There were candles burning and a few pine branches were artfully arranged as the centerpiece. "I love the smell of pine."

"Me too. So, how do you like your steak cooked?"

"Medium rare, please. Can I help you with anything?" Ryker asked.

"No, I've got it under control."

"I'm a great cook, you know," Ryker said, a smile teasing the corner of his lips.

"Oh, really? A man who can cook? Will wonders never cease?" she said with a mischievous smile of her own.

He let out a hearty laugh. "What? Men in the big city can't cook?"

Megan grabbed the steaks and put them under the broiler. "Well, in my experience, I haven't met a man yet who can cook. So color me surprised to hear that you can."

"Maybe you haven't met the right man yet?"

Megan looked at him with those big blue eyes and the impulse to kiss her was overwhelming, but he had to play it cool. She was being flirty with him and that was a good sign. At the very least, she liked him. It took all the will power he possessed not to pull her into his arms.

"Maybe you're right," she said with a soft chuckle. "Can you grab the salad in the fridge?"

"Yes, ma'am." He stepped over to the refrigerator and pulled out the two plates. "These look good," he said, bringing them to the table.

Megan had brought their wine to the table and was already sitting. Ryker joined her and they delved into the first course. When the stove dinged, she got up and turned the steaks over.

Ryker couldn't think of a nicer dinner he'd ever had. Their conversation flowed easily and there were none of those awkward pauses many new couples experience when first dating. He was impressed with how well she had done in her career and he told her bits and pieces about his former military career. That was something he didn't want to talk too much about and she didn't press him on that.

"That was absolutely delicious," he said, after swallowing the last bite. "Those steaks were cooked to perfection."

"Thank you, but now you owe me a dinner," Megan teased.

A smile split Ryker's face. "It would be my absolute pleasure," he said, raising his glass. "Shall we toast?"

"What are we toasting to?" she asked, raising her own wine glass.

"To a new beginning." He gently clinked his glass to hers, never taking his eyes off her.

After a moment's pause, she said, "To a new beginning."

"Megan, I really want—" A loud alert' on Ryker's phone interrupted their perfect moment. He pulled the phone from his belt and looked at the screen. Alarm swept over his face. "Sorry, I've got to go," he said, jumping up from the table. He grabbed his coat and rushed out the door before Megan had a chance to ask him what was wrong. He felt awful leaving her like that, but he'd had no choice.

As the truck raced down the road, all Ryker could think about was Megan. Their evening had been wonderful. It was the first time in a long time that he'd enjoyed a romantic dinner with a beautiful woman. "Bad timing, Mrs. Bracken. Very bad timing," he mumbled as he stepped on the gas, speeding toward town.

Chapter 8

MEGAN SAT STARING AT THE FRONT door. What had just happened? Why did Ryker rush out of here? She'd been enjoying herself immensely and, for the first time in months, felt a stirring in her belly. Could she be falling for the handsome storeowner already? He was everything she'd been looking for—kind, considerate, a good conversationalist, supposedly a good cook, and one of the most handsome men she'd ever seen. There was an inner strength about him and she admired that a great deal. She loved the way he laughed at her silly jokes. What had he been going to say before he rushed out? His words replayed in her head. "Megan, I want to..."

Want to, what?

Want to kiss me, perhaps?

She had fantasized about kissing him all afternoon as she had prepared dinner and gathered the pine for the table centerpiece. She was hoping he felt the same way. The setting had been perfect—a candlelit dinner, soft music playing in the background, and a fire roaring in the fireplace. She couldn't have done anything more to set a romantic atmosphere, but here she sat.

Alone.

Again.

"What's a girl have to do to be kissed these days," she murmured as she stood and started clearing the table. "Oh crap. I forgot to get his cell number again." Maybe that wasn't so bad after all. It would mean another trip into town, where she hoped to find out what had sent Ryker racing out of her cabin. It had been so sudden and she hoped nothing awful had happened. She didn't know enough about him yet to try and figure out what could have happened that would cause him to leave so suddenly.

After washing the dishes, Megan poured herself another glass of wine before settling on the couch in front of the cozy fire. She hadn't expected to be sitting here by herself tonight, but there was no sense in letting the fire go to waste. She watched the fire dance as it devoured the logs and thought about Ryker. Was she opening herself up to more heartache by wanting to spend time with him? He had a life here and hers was two hours away. Could a long-distance relationship work? She didn't know, but if she had a sexy guy like Ryker waiting for her, a two-hour drive on the weekends would certainly be worth a try. That's if he even wanted to spend time with her.

The next day, Megan drove into town. She hadn't slept well, and when she did finally fall asleep, she dreamed of kissing Ryker. Dreams were wonderful, but it made her crave the real thing even more. After parking the car near the general store, she bounded up the steps, hoping to see Ryker behind the counter. What greeted her was something entirely different. The CLOSED sign still hung on the door. She leaned her forehead on the glass, trying to see inside, but it was too dark to see anything or anyone. Ryker wasn't here. That seemed strange especially since it was the only store around for miles.

"Why didn't I get his cell number?" she chastised herself. She hadn't gotten his number because she was too busy staring at him and fantasizing about his soft sultry kisses. She vowed the first thing she was going to ask him the next time she saw him was for his cell number. There would be no more driving into town just to talk to him, and boy, did she want to talk to him. That sexy deep voice of his floated over her skin sending shivers down her spine and a fluttering in her chest.

With nothing more to be done at the store, she walked to the coffee house and ordered a hot vanilla latte and a blueberry scone. The shop was busy with customers. There were multiple couples, young and old, nestled together on couches and at the bistro tables. There was one table open by the window and Megan sat down. At least she'd be able to see if Ryker drove by.

She lingered over her latte for another thirty minutes, but Ryker didn't driven by or open up the store. Time for Plan B. She'd go to the bookstore and immerse herself in finding new treasures. That should eat up at least an hour or two. Surely, by then, Ryker would be at the store.

Plan B was an utter failure. She couldn't concentrate on the books when thoughts of Ryker filled her mind. Where was he? No one seemed to know, although she did find out that it was unusual for him not to open the store. Locals told her they could set their watch by the store opening and closing each day. What was going on? Where was he?

There was no Plan C and no more places to go in town to wait for him. What could be so important that it kept him from opening the store especially this week? There was always last minute purchases for a Christmas dinner and the general store was well stocked in anticipation. She had no idea where the next grocery store was located around here.

Megan sighed and trudged back to her car. She had thought she wanted the solitude of the cabin this Christmas season, but after meeting Ryker, she realized that she would like nothing better than to share a cup of eggnog with him on Christmas Day. "To a new beginning," he had said at their cozy dinner together. Did he mean a new beginning with her? It was certainly what she had meant when she had toasted her glass with him.

She was sullen as she drove back to the cabin, and even the lively Christmas songs playing on the radio didn't pull her out of her funk. With no way to contact Ryker, she spent the rest of the day going over briefs she had brought with her. If nothing else, it made the time pass, but every time she looked at the dining table centerpiece, she was reminded of their one perfect dinner together. She didn't want it to be only one perfect dinner. She wanted lots and lots of dinners with him.

She made herself a light supper and sat on the couch, staring into the fire, daydreaming about Ryker. The hours stretched by, the fire died out, and without any word from Ryker, there was nothing left to do but go to bed. Megan sighed as she climbed under the covers. Where was he? What could be keeping him away? Surely by tomorrow, he'd be back at the store. She would try again tomorrow to see the hunky storeowner.

The next day was a repeat of the previous one. She drove to town, the CLOSED sign was still up, so she got her latte and scone and waited. Ryker didn't drive by, but as she left the coffee shop and walked to her car, she saw a customer go into the store. The store was open? He was here? Her feet raced down the street and she burst through the door and looked behind the counter. She was disappointed when she saw an older guy manning the register.

"Ummm, is Ryker around?" she asked him as he separated the bills in the cash register.

"Don't know. Just got a call to open up the store, that's all," he said without looking up.

"I see. Did he say when he was coming back?"

The man shrugged. "Didn't say. Now, are you buying something, because there's a line of people waiting behind you?"

Megan looked over her shoulder. Sure enough, people were lined up with last minute purchases for their Christmas celebrations. "No, sorry. I don't need anything. Thanks."

"Merry Christmas, Miss," he said.

"Merry Christmas."

A lead weight settled around her heart as Megan left the store and headed home. She still had no answers regarding Ryker's sudden disappearance. It was Christmas Eve and he was nowhere in sight. It certainly wasn't the evening she had fantasized about. A single tear rolled down her cheek as she drove back to the cabin.

RYKER GLANCED AT HIS watch. It was already two p.m. on Christmas Eve and they were waiting for the release papers. It had been Mrs. Bracken's Life Alert alarm that had gone off the night he had been enjoying dinner with Megan. Something dreadful was going on and he hadn't even had time to explain to Megan why he was leaving so suddenly. When he got to Mrs. Bracken's home, she was lying on the floor and disoriented. He scooped her up in his arms, grabbed the afghan from the couch and put it around her when he had her buckled in his truck. The drive to the hospital was ninety minutes away. In the emergency room, she had been frightened being in a strange place and he had promised to stay with her while she was there.

The nurse bustled into the room. "Hi, Mrs. Bracken. How are you feeling today?"

"Good as new. I'm ready to go home."

"Excellent. The pacemaker that was inserted in your chest will prevent any more of those episodes."

Mrs. Bracken nodded. "That's good. I don't want to go through that again."

The nurse turned to Ryker. "Will you be taking her home?"

Ryker nodded. "Yes."

"I need to go over a few instructions with you and then you're free to go."

Twenty minutes later, Mrs. Bracken was being wheeled down to the lobby. Ryker had gone to get the truck and hopped out when he saw her waiting inside the lobby. The lobby doors swooshed open and he helped her step up into the cab of the truck.

"Thank you and Merry Christmas," Mrs. Bracken said to the orderly who had wheeled her downstairs.

"Merry Christmas, Ma'am."

With her seat belt buckled, Ryker tucked the blanket around her lap. "Are you warm enough?"

"Yes, thank you, dear. I don't know what I'd do without you."

"Well, you won't have to wonder, I'm here. Now, let's get you home."

The older woman reached over and clasped Ryker's hand before they drove off. "Thank you, Ryker, for everything. You're such a good man."

"You're welcome. It was my pleasure."

By the time he got her settled back in her home, it was nearly five o'clock. He drove over to the store as Ben was closing up. "Thanks so much for opening for me today. I really appreciate it. Mrs. Bracken took a nasty tumble, but she's good now."

Ben nodded. "Not a problem. Happy to help out. Today's cash is in the deposit bag. Had a really good day with all the last minute sales."

"Excellent. Did you take a turkey for yourself?"

"Yeah, the misses came by earlier today to get it."

"Well, don't be standing around here. Go join your family and thanks again. Merry Christmas, Ben."

"Merry Christmas, Ryker" Ben said as he walked out the door.

Ryker grabbed the deposit bag and stuffed it in his coat pocket. He'd deal with that later, but first he had a surprise to pull off and he was running out of time. He went down the aisle to see what decorations he had left for Christmas. He was hoping there'd be a tree stand, ornaments and lights and cursed himself for not setting those aside earlier. There were only three packages of fifty-count lights left on the shelf, no tree stand and no ornaments. Guess Ben was right. It had been a great sales day. He grabbed the lights and headed out the door.

The next stop was the outdoor lot selling Christmas trees. He hoped Chris was still around. He parked his truck and went in search of a tree. There didn't seem to be too many left to choose from.

"Hey Ryker, can I help you find something? I was just getting ready to leave."

"Hi, Chris. I'm glad you're still here. I'm looking for maybe a five or six foot tree. Got any left?"

"Just a couple. They're over here," Chris said, leading the way. "There was more of a rush this afternoon than in past years.

As Ryker was following Chris, he spotted a beauty. "Hey, Chris. What about this one?"

The lot attendant turned around and chuckled. "That poor little tree has been here for the past two weeks. Guess no one wants a small tree this year."

Ryker walked around the tree. It was perfectly symmetrical, but only about four feet tall. "I do. I'll take it. How much do I owe you?"

Chris waved his hand. "Nothing, man. It's yours. Merry Christmas."

"Thanks. One more thing, do you have any flat pieces of wood I could use to make a tree stand?"

"Sure, come back to the office and we'll rig something up."

Sixty minutes later, Ryker was pulling into Megan's driveway, although he parked at the far end. He didn't want her to hear him until he was finished with his surprise. He opened up the tailgate and pulled out the spruce Christmas tree with the makeshift tree stand attached. He reached into the cab of the truck and pulled out the lights and began to wrap the strings around the tree. Finally, he went back to the truck and got the generator. He wanted everything to be perfect and set about surprising the woman who had so quickly stolen his heart.

He picked up the tree and generator and set them down outside the cabin's picture window. With a flick of a switch on the generator, the perfect little Christmas tree was ablaze with lights. He stood beside it and waited.

It didn't take long for the cabin door to open.

Ryker watched as Megan stepped out onto the porch. Her eyes widened in surprise and her hands flew to her mouth. By the look on her face, he had pulled off the perfect surprise.

"Oh my God!" she squealed. "It's so beautiful."

He walked to the porch as soft snowflakes began to fall, coating the branches of the tree. "I wanted to surprise you with a tree for Christmas. I noticed you hadn't gotten one when I was here for dinner the other night."

"You did all this for me?"

His hand caressed her cheek. "All for you, my dear, sweet Megan. Everyone deserves a second chance at happiness, especially at Christmas."

"I don't know what to say," she said as a tear spilled down her cheek.

"You don't have to say anything." He leaned down and gently kissed her sweet lips. A moan escaped her and he pulled her into his arms. When her lips parted, his tongue savored every inch of her mouth and he kissed her long and deep.

It was several moments before he released her. "I've wanted to do that since the first moment I laid eyes on you."

Megan smiled. "I felt the same. Thank you for making this the best Christmas I've had in a very long time."

"My pleasure," he said and pulled her back in his arms for another sensual kiss. "I'm sorry I ran out of here so fast the other night. It was Mrs. Bracken," he explained, telling Megan what had happened to the older woman.

"You're such a good man and I'm so very happy you're here with me tonight."

"So am I," he said. He couldn't believe his good fortune. Whether it was luck or fate, he didn't know, but he wasn't going to question it. All he knew was that he had found her—the perfect woman for him—and he wasn't going to waste another moment without letting her know that over and over again. His mouth covered hers and they shared another passionate kiss in the glow of the perfect little Christmas tree.

Megan shivered and Ryker reluctantly let her go. "We should go inside. You'll catch a cold standing out here."

"What about the tree? Can we bring it inside?"

"Of course. Let me just shut down the generator. I'll be right in."

Megan went inside and pushed a table aside to make room for the tree near the window. "You can put it over there," she said when Ryker carried the tree inside.

"Do you have an extension cord?" he asked.

Megan nodded, walked to the kitchen and pulled one out of the drawer. "Here you go," she said, handing him the cord. "Would you like a glass of wine?"

"Yes. That would be great."

With the tree glowing and the fire warming the room, Megan put the glasses of wine on the coffee table. Ryker soon joined her on the couch.

"Were you surprised?" he asked.

"It was the best surprise I've ever had," she said, handing him a wine glass. She held hers up for a toast. "To a very good beginning."

Ryker clinked her glass. "Yes, to a very good beginning."

Megan took a sip of wine before setting her glass down. "I have a confession to make."

"Really? What kind of a confession?"

Megan was wringing her hands and he couldn't imagine what was making her so nervous. "I thought I'd done something to scare you off especially when you weren't at the store the yesterday."

Ryker shook his head. "I'm so sorry about running out of here like that. I had wanted more than anything to kiss you that night."

"You did?"

"Oh, yes. It's all I've been thinking about for the past two days."

"You're not alone in that," she said, leaning toward him. "No more thinking. How about you just kiss me?"

Ryker pulled her into his arms and his lips devoured hers, his tongue sliding over lips and tongue in perfect rhythm exploring every each of her mouth. His hand tangled in her hair and Megan moaned. When they finally parted, Ryker sat back and looked at her. "I've never felt anything so wonderful before. You're one special lady, Megan Duffy."

"Thank you. You're pretty special yourself," she said running her hand up his biceps.

"I know we've just met, but is there any chance you'll stick around these parts for a while."

"I had only planned to be up here for a few days, but I know my calendar is clear for the next two weeks.

Ryker nodded. "Hmm…two weeks, huh?"

"What does that mean?" she asked, confusion written on her face.

He caressed her cheek. "It means that in the next two weeks, I'll have to convince you to come back here over and over again."

Megan gave him a brilliant smile, one that spoke of hope and maybe, love. "I think that can be arranged, but first, I want to enjoy all this convincing you're going to do!"

Ryker chuckled. "Yes, ma'am. Your wish is my command," he said as he pulled her into his arms for another toe-curling kiss."

THE END

DEBRA ELIZABETH

Mistletoe
KISSES

A NEW ENGLAND ROMANCE

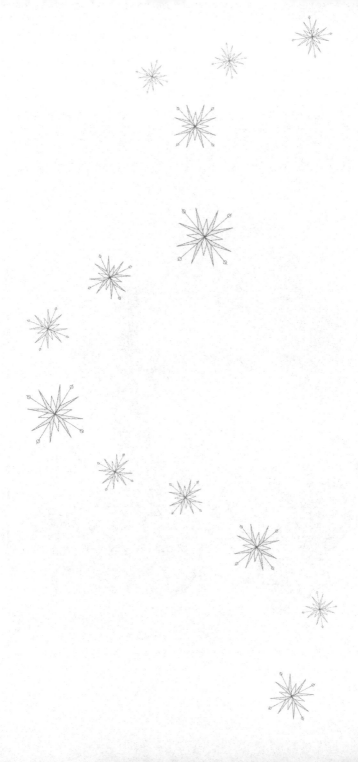

Chapter 1
Ellie

I LOOKED AROUND THE EASTERN STANDARD Bar for the third time, trying to pick out Danielle, one of my best friends, who was supposed to be here by now. If there's one thing you can say about Danielle, it's that she's habitually late. I was getting dirty looks from other patrons, who wanted the seat I was holding for her. The bar in the heart of Kendall Square in Boston was located between our workplaces and was a convenient place for us to meet for a drink or two after a long, hard day of work. I loved coming here, not so much for the drinks, which were good, but because they served a killer cherry-nectarine cobbler—my absolute favorite dessert.

Boy, did I need it tonight.

Danielle and I had been commiserating over the fact that neither of us have had any success in the dating scene as of late. What better way to commiserate than with drinks and a to-die-for dessert? I don't know why our recent dates had gone so badly, but after the last round of less-than-stellar ones, we had both decided on a moratorium on dating for a while. It amazed me that Danielle was having such a hard time finding a guy. She was gorgeous—five foot seven, curvy in a good way, blond hair, and striking green eyes. Who wouldn't want to date her? But that was the problem; guys wanted to date and bed her, but that was it. No commitment, no next date after a night of sex. What was wrong with those guys? Even if there was no sex on the first date, the guys failed to call her for second one. They only wanted to say they'd bedded a gorgeous blonde. Some guys were so shallow, and we seemed to have found every one of them.

I could understand why I hadn't had any luck finding someone special, especially when I hung out with my friends. At five foot two, I looked like the little sister tagging along behind the big kids. Although my college friends never made me feel that way, my own insecurity made me shrink inside myself whenever we went out together. Why would any guy want to talk to the girl with curly brown hair that was out of control most of the time when there were four other, gorgeous girls to choose from? I felt like I attracted the leftovers—the men that didn't stand a chance in hell with my friends.

When I hung out with Danielle, though, the dynamics shifted a bit, and I felt like I didn't get overshadowed quite as much. Danielle was a hometown type of girl, having been raised somewhere in the Midwest. All those states kind of blended together for me, and I could never remember whether it was Kansas, Missouri, or Iowa she hailed from. I probably should have paid more attention to geography in school.

I glanced at the door again and was worried I wouldn't be able to hold the seat at the bar much longer when I finally saw her weaving her way through the crowd.

"I'm sorry I'm late," she said. "Last-minute phone call. I couldn't get the client off the phone quick enough."

"I figured it was something like that."

Danielle put her purse on the seat I was saving and leaned toward me. "I have to pee. Be right back." She straightened and turned to leave, bumping into a guy holding two beers. The beers tipped and spilled all over the front of his shirt.

"Oh my god, I'm so sorry. I didn't see you," she said.

The guy looked up and gave her the sexiest smile. "Not a problem."

"I feel terrible about this. Let me buy you two more," Danielle said, signaling the bartender.

"How about you let me buy you a drink instead?" he asked.

"What about the beers?

The guy poured the remainder of one beer into the other glass. "Let me get this to my friend. You won't run away on me now, will you?"

Danielle shook her head. "I'll be here."

I saw the instant spark of interest between those two and had a feeling that our moratorium on dating would be over before it even began.

So much for our pact.

Just as I had predicted, those two were hitting it off, and suddenly, I felt like a third wheel. I didn't want to hang around especially if Danielle really was into this guy. I leaned toward her. "Hey, I'm going to get going. You okay here with him?" I whispered.

"Sure. I'll be fine and will call you over the weekend."

I said my goodbyes and headed out the door. No sense hanging around, especially when a nice, hot bath was calling my name. It had been a long week and all I wanted was to go home.

Danielle was true to her word and called me on Sunday gushing about Steve. She talked nonstop for twenty minutes about him.

"So, I gather you like this guy?" I asked, knowing full well she did from what I had witnessed at the bar Friday night.

"Yeah. He's pretty special."

I was happy for my friend, but a little sad too, knowing I had probably lost my Friday night drinking partner. I wasn't planning on hanging out with Danielle and Steve, especially not when their budding romance was so new.

Not even a year after they first met, I was standing in the church for Danielle and Steve's wedding day. Since that first meeting last summer, they had been inseparable. I was thrilled that Danielle had found the love of her life, even if it meant we didn't get together as much as we used to, but that was the way of things with new romances.

That first blush of love overruled everything, even good friendships. Maybe some day, I'd know that kind of love, but my options didn't look very good at the moment.

I looked over my shoulder at the group gathering behind me. Wonderful. Another wedding—fifth one in two years, and boy did my finances ever know it. There was the money I'd spent on various dresses, shoes, and bridal showers, and I wondered what I would do with another full-length chiffon gown. When I hung them all together in my closet, it looked like a rainbow—five pastel-colored dresses, good for only one day. It didn't matter what each bride said—"you'll be able to wear it again"—I knew the truth of it. These dresses would eventually go to Goodwill or one of those prom dress promotions that dry cleaners held. At least they'd be out of my closet.

I shouldn't complain though. Those events had been for my closest friends—my gorgeous, statuesque college friends that I would do anything for, even buy another chiffon dress. Why they were friends with me, I'd never understand. Maybe I was the comic relief of the group? All I could think of throughout our college years was that one of these things was not like the others.

As I waited for the procession to begin, I heard one of the groomsmen say, "Jared's plane was delayed. He won't make it for another hour."

"We can't wait any longer," Danielle said. She turned toward me. "Sorry, Ellie, but you'll have to walk by yourself. You don't mind, do you?"

Of course I minded, especially since I'd look like a junior bridesmaid walking in front of all the grown-ups, but I didn't want my disappointment to ruin Danielle's wedding. It was a beautiful Saturday in May—not too warm, not too cold—and I wasn't going to be the one to throw cold water on the event. "No problem," I told her. "Let's get this show on the road!"

Danielle hugged me. "Thank you for being such a good friend."

"You're welcome. Whatever you need, I'm happy to oblige."

The rest of the bridal party lined up behind me, each bridesmaid paired with her respective husband. I heard the music begin, took a deep breath, and began the long walk down the aisle.

The ceremony was poignant—the bride was marrying the love of her life and from the way Steve looked at her, I could tell he felt the same way. Who could have predicted that a chance meeting at the Eastern Standard Bar last summer would end here? Their personal vows were spoken, the rings were exchanged, and there wasn't a dry eye in the church when husband and wife kissed.

The usual picture taking happened after the ceremony, and then it was time for the introductions at the reception. I asked Danielle to let me slip into the reception without being announced. Not going to happen, however.

"Ellie, you're important to me. I want everyone to know that," Danielle said.

I shrugged, and when my name was announced, I walked in as fast as my short legs could carry me and scurried over to the head table. I'd never been so happy to see everyone seated and the food served. I was starving and dug into my salad, only to have my attempt to stuff myself interrupted by the best man's speech. Forgot about that. I reluctantly put my fork down and waited while the speeches droned on. My stomach was rumbling and I hoped no one could hear it. Finally, all the speeches were over and I could enjoy my meal.

After the delicious dinner was finished and the dishes were cleared away, I sat at the head table with my chin cupped in my hand and watched the rest of the bridal party take to the dance floor with the bride and groom. Everyone looked so happy, and why shouldn't they? My friends had each found their own happy ending; even Danielle, who had complained about the lack of good guys out there just last year. We had promised to stay single together. Well, that didn't last long. Danielle was happily smiling at her husband as he swept her around the dance floor.

A long sigh slipped through my lips. Really, where were all the good guys? Surely Danielle couldn't have scooped up the last available bachelor in the Boston area, could she? Maybe I'd have to try one of those dating sites again, although I shuddered at the prospect of going on blind date after blind date with strangers. In my brief experience with those sites, disaster was too kind a word to describe the dates I'd gone on.

A shadow crept over me, and a hand appeared in front of my face.

"I believe this is my dance," said a deep baritone voice.

I looked up into the most beautiful crystal-blue eyes I'd ever seen. It took me several moments to stop staring at the guy standing by the head table and answer him. This was it—my chance to say something clever and witty. "Oh?"

That was brilliant and sure to sweep any guy off his feet! When did I lose the ability to put two sentences together?

"Yes. I'm the wayward groomsman. Shall we join the bridal party on the dance floor?"

I nodded and stood, but when I took a step toward him, my shoe caught in the hem of my dress and I stumbled into his arms. Luckily for me, he had strong arms and caught me before I did a faceplant on the floor.

"Whoa. Most women wait at least five minutes before they throw themselves at me," he said with a chuckle.

Oh great! What a way to make a first impression. Maybe I am the comic relief after all.

"Well, I'm not most women," I said with as much dignity as I could muster, seeing as I wasn't fully upright yet.

"Touché! By the way, I'm Jared Castian."

I disentangled myself from Jared and said, "Nice to meet you, Jared. Sorry about falling into your arms. My shoe got caught in my dress." Now I was rambling, but I couldn't stop myself. Jared had unnerved me and that was unusual for me. I didn't usually get tongue-tied around guys I've just met.

"Not a problem. And who am I dancing with?"

I chuckled. Not only had I thrown myself into his arms, but I hadn't even told him my name. I wondered if I should even bother. He was probably only here for the wedding, and I was sure that a good-looking guy like him already had a girlfriend. There was absolutely no way he'd take a second look at me, but then again, what did I have to lose? Might as well enjoy an afternoon of dancing with a handsome stranger. It was certainly better than the alternative—sitting at the head table by myself all evening. "Hi, Jared. I'm Ellie Davidson."

"Shall we, Ellie?"

I nodded and took his extended hand. Immediate warmth flooded through me and an unexpected thrill raced up my spine. That was something new. I'd never felt anything like it before. Talk about instant attraction. Was this how Danielle had felt when she first met Steve? I stole a look at Jared as we made our way around the tables to the dance floor—strong chiseled jawline, broad shoulders, and full, sensual lips. He wasn't too tall, probably five foot nine or ten, which suited me fine, but it was his eyes that captivated me. He had the kind of eyes a girl could get lost in, and I was more than happy to be lost for the afternoon.

When we reached the dance floor, he pulled me into his arms, and we began a slow circuit around the other couples. As we neared the bride and groom, I saw Steve's face light up.

"You're here! I thought you were a no-show when I heard your plane was delayed."

Jared nodded. "Me too, but then it all worked out, and here I am. Danielle, it's a pleasure to meet you."

Danielle smiled. "I've heard a lot about you."

"Really? All good, I hope."

"So far, but I think there're more stories that Steve hasn't told me yet. You two were quite the pair growing up from what I hear."

Steve chuckled. "That we were, my love. Jared, we need to catch up. It's been too long. How long are you in town for?"

"Just today, but I'll be back soon."

"Yeah?"

"Being transferred to Boston."

"Great," Steve said, giving Jared a high five. "Let me know when you're back, and we can catch up over a few beers."

"You got it."

As I listened to their conversation, my heart did a little pitter-patter. Jared was moving here. Could I dare to hope that he'd want to see me again?

"So, when are you moving here?" I asked, taking a chance that I wasn't being too forward.

"June one. The company wants me to oversee an upcoming merger."

"What do you do?

"Corporate lawyer."

Color me impressed. Trying to keep the conversation going but not be too pushy, I weighed my next words carefully. "So, do you have a place to live?"

Jared quirked an eyebrow at me. "Why? Are you offering your place?"

His response startled me until I saw his lips turn up in a boyish grin and those gorgeous eyes twinkle with amusement. "Oh, I see. You're a funny boy, too," I said.

He chuckled. "Sorry, couldn't help myself. You looked so earnest, like you were saving a lost puppy or something."

"I wasn't trying to pry, you know." *Well, maybe a little.* "By the way, I would definitely save a lost puppy."

"Yes, I believe you would," he said as he pulled me closer. "But I don't need saving."

Chapter 2
Jared

I DIDN'T LIKE TO ADMIT IT, but I hadn't been looking forward to Steve's wedding. Work was crazy and I'd wanted to use the weekend to wrap up some details, but Steve was one of my best friends, and I couldn't skip out on his big day. Everything changed the moment I spotted the brunette sitting alone at the head table. It was like an invisible thread was drawing me to her. When I got closer, her expressive brown eyes wowed me. With a few freckles sprinkled across her nose and cheeks, she was the prettiest girl I'd seen in a long time. I wasn't into the usual "tall and stick-like beauty" standard, and that was all I seemed to be around at the law firm. I wanted someone who didn't see everything as a competition and who could make me laugh. Ellie had accomplished that before she uttered a single word. I loved a girl with a sense of humor.

Her tripping on her gown was the perfect excuse for me to hold her in my arms, and I took my time releasing her. She felt like she belonged there, and I didn't want to let her go. That was entirely new to me. I'd always been somewhat aloof when it came to dating. I was a busy lawyer and didn't want to invest the time and effort in the dating scene. It was a hassle I could do without. Guess it took the right girl to spark my interest. Ellie was adorable, she intrigued me, and I wanted to get to know her better. At least dancing gave me a good excuse to keep her close.

When the song ended, I asked, "Would you like a drink?"

"Sure. That would be nice." She nodded, and her rich brown curls bobbed as she stepped out of my arms.

I wasn't sure if I should take her hand. I didn't want to appear too forward, but I wanted to touch her again. Her skin was warm and smooth, and her small hand had fit perfectly in mine. Why not take a chance? It was worth the risk. I grasped her hand and leaned toward her. "I don't want anyone to snatch you away."

She giggled, a sweet, lyrical sound. "I don't think you have anything to worry about," she said as we walked toward the bar.

We waited our turn and finally made it to the front of the line. "What would you like?" I asked.

"Cosmopolitan would be great."

"Dry martini, two olives, and a cosmopolitan," I told the bartender.

"Coming right up."

"I know you're not a friend of the groom—I'd definitely remember meeting you. So you must be a friend of the bride."

"Yeah. I met her and all the bridesmaids in college, and we've been friends ever since. How long have you known Steve?"

"We grew up together." I grabbed the drinks, and we headed back to the head table. I put the drinks down and pulled out her chair before taking the seat next to her.

"Really? Where was that?" Ellie asked.

"St. Paul, Minnesota. Ever been?"

Ellie shook her head. Could she be any more desirable? I reached over and pushed a wayward curl behind her ear. "It was a great childhood, but both Steve and I couldn't wait to leave."

"Really?"

"I got accepted at Georgetown and Steve headed to CalTech, and we never looked back. We've gotten together as often as we could over the years. I'm thrilled he found the perfect girl." Another slow song began to play, and I held out my hand. "Care to dance again?"

I'm not usually the warm and fuzzy type, but her smile lit up her face, and I couldn't help but smile in response.

"Yes, I'd love to," she said.

I led her to the dance floor and pulled her into my arms. She felt wonderful as her body molded to mine as if she was made especially for me, and I wanted the song to play on all night. I held her tight, drinking in her sweet scent of orange blossoms. "You smell so good," I murmured in her ear.

"You like it? It's Nerola by Pacifica. First time I smelled it, I fell in love with it. Such a sweet, light fragrance."

"It suits you."

The DJ played three slow songs in a row, and it felt wonderful dancing with Ellie. I inwardly groaned when he decided to change things up. I reluctantly let her go as the oldie but goodie, YMCA, blared out of the speakers.

"Oh, I love this song," she said. She immediately lined up with the other bridesmaids, and they went through the dance motions, laughing and giggling together. "Care to join us?" she asked, holding out her hand.

"No, thanks. I'll sit this one out," I said before making my way back to the table." I took a seat and enjoyed my martini, but I couldn't take my eyes off Ellie. Out of the corner of my eye, I saw Steve headed my way. I stood and shook his hand. "Congrats, man. Danielle is a beautiful girl."

"She is, and everything I've been looking for."

"Where are you guys heading for the honeymoon?" I asked.

"Aruba for ten days."

"Nice. Let's get together when you get back. I should be up here by then."

"Sounds good. It was great to see you. It's been too long."

"I agree, but soon I'll be up here in Boston. It will certainly make it easier to get together."

"Fantastic."

When Steve left to rejoin his bride, I looked around for Ellie but couldn't see her anywhere. Where did she go? Hopefully, she hadn't left, especially since I hadn't gotten her number yet. I breathed a sigh of relief when I saw her reenter the reception hall. I wasn't going to take any more chances that she'd slip away again and made my way over to her. Before I reached her, one of the other groomsmen grabbed her hand and dragged her out on the floor joining the rest of the bridal party dancing. I felt a momentary pang of jealousy. Whoa—where did that come from? I'd just met this girl, and yet, already I was feeling possessive of her time. This was an entirely new emotion for me, although I somehow didn't mind it as much as I thought I should.

When the song ended, she came back to the head table and sat next to me. Her face was flushed a rosy pink, and she looked positively radiant.

"You looked good out there."

She laughed and sipped her Cosmopolitan. "Wow, you must have been watching someone else! My friends dance so much better than I do."

"Do they? I only had eyes for you. Any chance I can have your number?"

Chapter 3
Ellie

I ALMOST CHOKED ON MY DRINK. Did I hear Jared correctly? He wanted my phone number? Now that was something I hadn't seen coming. I had hoped, of course, that he could be interested in me, but hoping didn't usually work out for me. "You want my number?"

"I do." He pulled out his phone and handed it to me. "Want to do the honors?"

I took his phone with trembling fingers. "Sure," I said and entered my information. I regretted leaving my phone at home because it would have been a perfect opportunity to get Jared's number as well. Now I'd have to be content with giving him my number, at least until the first time he called.

What if he never called? What if he was just being nice? He won't call. The nice guys never do! I had to stop my old insecurities from rearing their ugly heads. If he wasn't planning to call, he never would have asked for my number in the first place, right?

"Here you go," I said, handing him back the phone. Before we had a chance to talk any more, the DJ announced that it was time to cut the cake. I was eager to see if Steve would be stupid enough to smash the cake into my friend's face. Danielle had told us girls earlier that she'd warned him about doing that, but guys are dumb. If Steve wanted to enjoy his honeymoon, he had better toe the line.

I leaned toward Jared. "Let's see how smart Steve is," I whispered.

Jared furrowed his brow. "What? Steve is one of the smartest guys I know."

"Just wait. You'll see." I held my breath as the piece of cake was cut. Steve broke off a smaller piece and offered it to his bride. Danielle smiled, and he fed her with all the grace of a gentleman. She did the same with him, and I finally exhaled.

"What was so special about that?" Jared asked.

"Guys can be stupid sometimes. You see those ridiculous videos of grooms smashing wedding cake all over the bride. Danielle told Steve not to do that, but I think we were all holding our breath to see if he'd take her wishes seriously. Lucky for him, he did; otherwise, it could have been a chilly honeymoon."

Jared smiled. "I told you Steve was a smart guy."

I chuckled as the servers came out with trays loaded with wedding cake. There were three different flavors—

chocolate, lemon, and strawberry. I opted for a lemon piece, and Jared asked for chocolate.

As he cut a piece of his cake, he asked, "Care to taste?"

After the conversation we'd just had, I wasn't sure if he was trying to be funny. I didn't want to end up with cake on my face, so I declined. "No, thanks. I'm happy with lemon."

Jared popped the piece into his mouth. "Mmmm, you don't know what you're missing. This is delicious."

Now he'd gone and done it. I loved chocolate cake and was dying for a taste. Before he could offer again, I held up my fork. "May I?"

He gave me a slow and sexy smile as butterflies tickled my insides. "How about this? You give me a piece of lemon, and I'll give you a piece of chocolate," he said as he scooped another piece of cake on his fork.

"Sure." All I could think of was watching the lemon cake slide past those luscious lips. I cut a piece and offered it to him. He parted his lips and some of the frosting smeared on them. Before I thought about what I was doing, my lips pressed against his. I didn't usually kiss men I'd just met, but there was something special about Jared. I knew that if I didn't kiss him, I'd regret it, especially if I never heard from him again. His lips were soft and inviting. My heart hammered in my chest, and a fierce, unexpected arousal rocked me to my core. I reluctantly sat back and licked the frosting off my lips.

"My turn," he said, his eyes flashing as he slid a piece of cake into my mouth. When his hands cupped my face, I was ready for another kiss.

I nearly melted in his arms when his tongue brushed against my mouth. My lips parted, and an intense thrill raced through me as his tongue slowly and expertly explored every inch of my mouth. His searing kiss was the only thing in my world at the moment. I shut everything else out—the noise, the music, and the bride preparing to throw the bouquet. It was perfect until someone yelled my name.

Jared broke the kiss first. "Seems like you're being paged."

I was numb, and it took me a minute to come back down to earth. "What?"

Jared pointed to the dance floor, where Danielle was waiting to throw her bouquet.

"Ellie, come down here," she shouted.

As much as I loved Danielle, her timing was horrible. I didn't want to go down to the floor and watch her throw the flowers. I wanted to stay in my own little fairytale world, where Jared had eyes only for me. But I had no choice, and I looked at Jared and shrugged. "Duty calls. I'll be right back."

I stood in the back of the line hoping to get back to Jared as quick as possible. I watched the bouquet sailed through the air. As luck or fate would have it, I reached up and caught it, much to the disappointment of the other single gals.

Danielle was thrilled and gave me a hug. "I'm glad it was you," she whispered.

"Seems like that bouquet had a mind of its own. I thought for sure someone in front would have grabbed it."

"Now, you know what this means, right?" she asked.

I groaned and said, "Come on, don't start that again. I don't even have a boyfriend."

The rest of the bridesmaids surrounded me, all shouting, "Ellie is next!"

I had to laugh at their enthusiasm, but I was anxious to slip back to the table and spend more time with Jared. No such luck. The DJ chose that moment to play "the chicken dance." None of us could resist. I put the bouquet down on the nearest table and joined in. It was such a silly dance, and everyone was laughing and having a good time. I couldn't see Jared, but I was hoping he wouldn't disappear before I had a chance to continue our kissing session. When the song ended, I grabbed the flowers and made a beeline back to the table, only to see that Jared was no longer there.

Damn, I wonder where he went? Was I being too pushy earlier, when I kissed him? Will he come back and continue our cake-eating session, or was that special moment lost in the hustle and bustle of the wedding?

The servers were more than efficient and both our pieces of cake had been cleared off the table. Talk about fast service. I wanted to eat some lemon cake and wondered if I could snag one of the servers and ask for another piece. If I couldn't be with Jared, at least I'd have my cake.

Chapter 4
Jared

IT FELT SO NATURAL TO cup Ellie's face and kiss her—a kiss so sweet and sensual that it stirred something deep within me. It had been such a long time since I'd felt that kind of attraction. I couldn't get enough of her and was disappointed when the bride called her away. I watched as she caught the bouquet, hoping she'd come back to the table. I definitely wanted to feed her more cake and kiss those luscious lips.

When the DJ started playing that silly dance song, I knew she'd be out on the dance floor for a while longer. I downed the rest of my martini and headed back to the bar, where I saw Steve and a bunch of his buddies, all throwing back beers.

Steve glanced my way and waved me over. "Hey man, I want to introduce you to the gang."

After the introductions were over and I had shaken hands with four other guys, Steve asked, "When do you officially move up here?"

"June 1. The firm has an apartment downtown that I'll be in for the near future. Why, what's up?"

"We have a poker night once a month. Care to join in?"

I nodded. "Absolutely."

"Great. I'll text you the details about the next game," Steve said.

"Thanks. Looking forward to it." I looked over at the head table, but there was no sign of Ellie yet. She was probably still dancing with her girlfriends. I stayed at the bar, shooting the breeze with the other guys, for a while before I remembered to glance at my watch. Unfortunately, I had to leave if I wanted to catch my shuttle back to Washington. It looked like I wouldn't be sharing any more cake with Ellie. That was a shame.

I slapped Steve on the back. "Listen, Steve. I'm glad I made it to your wedding, but duty calls. I've got to go. I have a lot of material to prepare for this big merger I'm overseeing."

Steve extended his hand. "Thanks for coming, man. It was great seeing you, and I look forward to taking your money at the next poker game."

I shook his hand and said, "Just try!"

I said my goodbyes to the other guys and took one last look at the head table. No luck, Ellie was still on the dance floor with her friends. I didn't want to intrude on their fun, but I wished I could have said goodbye to her and got in one last kiss before I left.

I slipped out of the reception and headed for my rental car. I figured I'd change at the airport. Didn't really want to fly in a tuxedo. I made it to Logan in record time. Not much traffic on a Saturday night. By the time I turned in the rental car, made it through security, and changed into something more comfortable, my flight was boarding.

Once I reached my seat, I pulled out my phone and scrolled through my contacts to find Ellie's number. I wanted to call her, but she probably wouldn't hear the phone ring; that's if she even had the phone with her at the reception. I had to settle for sending a text.

ENJOYED MEETING YOU. I'LL BE BACK IN BOSTON SOON. WILL CALL YOU.

I switched the phone to airplane mode and settled in my seat, thinking about the petite brunette who had captured my undivided attention. I loved the way she laughed, the way she danced with abandon, and most especially, the way she kissed. Was her impetuous nature part of her personality or had the free-flowing alcohol at the wedding loosened her up? It didn't matter to me one way or another because I had enjoyed her spontaneity. Who would have guessed she'd kiss me first? That was a nice surprise. I was glad she did because I'd been getting ready to do the same, only she'd beaten me to the punch. I smiled for no particular reason except that I was thinking about Ellie. I wanted more than a brief afternoon of dancing with her and couldn't wait until I was back in Boston. I was definitely planning to call her.

Chapter 5
Ellie

WHILE I WAS WAITING FOR my first dental patient to arrive, I pulled out my phone and reread Jared's text, which he'd sent me a week ago, after Danielle's wedding. The same thrill raced through me each and every time I read it. I was a little disappointed I hadn't heard from him again, but I knew he was probably busy at work, getting ready for the transfer. I couldn't wait until he was in Boston. Hopefully, I'd be hearing from him any day now.

I glanced at the wall calendar—May 25, another week to go before he transfers up here. I tried not to put too much stock in his text, just in case he was merely being polite, but I sure hoped he meant what he wrote because I was definitely looking forward to seeing him again. I couldn't help but smile when I relived our kiss. It had been the best kiss I'd ever had and I definitely wanted more of those sexy lips.

I put my phone on silent, slid it into my pocket, and went to greet my eight o'clock patient. My day was jam-packed with patients, and by the time I got home twelve hours later, the only thing I was looking forward to was a long hot soak in the tub and a glass of wine.

As I emptied my pockets, I realized I'd forgotten to take my phone off silent on the way home. I stared at the phone, shocked to realize I had another text from Jared.

CAME UP TO BOSTON EARLY. YOU UP FOR DINNER TONIGHT?

Oh no! I can't believe I missed it. I'd been so busy with patients today that I hadn't even felt the phone vibrate in my pocket. I was totally bummed and, all of a sudden, not very tired. I answered his text with an apology for missing his earlier message.

SO SORRY. DIDN'T SEE YOUR MESSAGE UNTIL NOW.

I didn't hold out much hope that he'd respond this late.

My phone dinged almost immediately.

NO WORRIES. HOW ABOUT TOMORROW NIGHT?

That familiar thrill surged through me again. I didn't want to text anymore; I wanted to hear his sexy baritone voice. Would he think me too forward if I called him instead? I hoped not because I really wanted to talk to him. I clicked on the "details" link and tapped the phone icon. My heart was hammering in my chest with the anticipation of talking to him again.

"Castian."

I was momentarily thrown by his reply, but quickly recovered. "Hey, Jared. It's Ellie."

"Can I call you right back?"

"Sure," I said and hung up. That was not the response I'd been hoping for, and I wondered if I had made a mistake by calling him. He'd sounded annoyed when he answered the phone, but I rationalized that he was the one who texted me first. What if he was one of those guys who hated talking on the phone? Had I ruined our fledging relationship before it even had a chance to flourish? My mind kept going back and forth between "what ifs" and "should haves," and when the phone rang, I nearly jumped out of my skin, dropping the phone in the process.

I bent down and scooped it off the floor. "Hello."

"Hey, Ellie, sorry about that. Had to finish up with another call."

"Not a problem," I lied, mostly because I didn't think he'd want to hear about my inner dialogue. "Sorry for not responding to your text earlier. I was really busy at work today and didn't even see it until a few minutes ago."

"I had hoped that was the case," he said in his sexy baritone voice, "and you weren't just ignoring me."

"No. I definitely wasn't ignoring you."

"So, you didn't answer my question."

"Oh?"

"Are you free tomorrow night for dinner?" he asked.

"Yes. Dinner would be great."

"Where do you live? Should I send a car for you?"

That was odd? A car? Was this guy rich or something? Who sends a car for a date? "Um, I could just meet you somewhere."

"Do you have a favorite restaurant you'd like to go to?"

"Not really. I don't go into Boston much these days. Where are you staying?"

"660 Washington Street."

"Oh my, fancy address."

"It's the firm's apartment, and it's actually pretty small. Believe me, there's nothing to be impressed about. What kind of food do you like?"

"Seafood is my favorite."

"Okay, I'll find a place and text you the address."

"That sounds fine. I'm actually off tomorrow, so whatever time you choose is good."

"Really?"

"Yes. Why?"

"I have meetings until noon, but then I'm free. I'd love to spend the afternoon with you, if you'd like that?"

I swallowed the lump in my throat. "You would?"

"Of course, don't sound so surprised. I'll call you tomorrow when I'm free, and we can spend the afternoon together. Does that work for you?"

"That sounds wonderful. Talk to you tomorrow. Bye."

"Bye, and Ellie?"

"Yes?"

"Thanks for calling me. It was great to hear your voice again."

I stood in the middle of my living room, grinning like a fool, until I heard the call click off. Jared wanted to see me again. Could my heart beat any faster with delicious anticipation? I could hardly wait for the chance to kiss him again. I closed my eyes and relived our kiss at the wedding, something I'd done more times than I could count, but this time, it was different. I would actually see him tomorrow, and hopefully, that would include lots more kissing.

I was floating on cloud nine as I made my way into the bathroom for that long, hot soak. I let the tub fill while I brushed my teeth. When I finally slipped into the soothing water, a contented sigh escaped my lips. Oh yes, this was heaven, or at least pretty close to it. I leaned back, closed my eyes, and relived that cake-kissing session with Jared once more.

Chapter 6
Jared

I WAS GLAD ELLIE HAD CALLED me. I'd wondered whether she was ignoring me when I didn't get a response to my text. Although I was disappointed not to have dinner with her tonight, spending tomorrow afternoon and evening with her instead would more than make up for it.

Not being familiar with Boston, I did a quick internet search for "seafood restaurants." Legal Harborside popped up first, and after looking at the photos and the menu, I decided it was the perfect place to take Ellie for our first date. Then I searched for things to do in Boston and came up with what I hoped would be an enjoyable way to spend the day. After another few hours of work, I hit the sack. My last thought before sleep claimed me was of Ellie and her sweet lips.

The next day dawned with a brilliant blue sky and a few puffy clouds that looked like cotton batting floating

194

across the sky. I spent the morning taking care of business and finished around noon. Then I called Ellie, who picked up on the second ring.

"Hello."

"Hi Ellie. It's Jared."

"Hi. How'd your meeting go?"

"Fine. Still want to go out?"

"Of course. Where should I meet you?"

"Actually, I'll come and get you. Parking could prove difficult where we're going. What's your address?"

She gave me her address and then asked, "What should I wear? Does it matter?"

"I'm sure you'll look great in whatever you wear. Make sure you're comfortable, though, because I plan to spend as much time as possible with you today."

"Oh, that sounds intriguing. Where exactly are you taking me?"

I had to chuckle at her persistence. "No hints. I'll be there soon. Bye."

"Bye."

I called for the car and headed downstairs to wait. Now that I had our itinerary planned, I couldn't wait to see her again. Within thirty-five minutes, I was ringing her doorbell. She opened the door and greeted me with a sweet, infectious smile.

She was dressed in a peach sundress that complemented her porcelain skin and hugged her curves to perfection. She looked even more beautiful than she had at Steve's wedding. "You look stunning." I wanted to pull her into my arms and kiss her senseless but decided to play it cool and let her make the first move. I didn't want to be too pushy and scare her away.

"Thank you. You look pretty good yourself," she said.

I extended my arm. "Are you hungry?"

She grabbed a white shrug and her purse before slipping her arm in mine. "Starving."

"Good. I hope you'll approve of my choice."

"Want to tell me where we're going?"

"No. I'd like it to be a surprise. Is that okay with you?"

"Sure."

I helped her into the back seat of the car and slipped in beside her. The driver knew our destination, so I was able to give Ellie my full attention. "Care for a glass of champagne?"

"Wow, you're pulling out all the stops. Color me impressed. I actually love champagne."

Having a small mini-bar in the limo was certainly convenient for setting a romantic mood. I popped the cork, poured two flutes, and handed one to Ellie.

"Thank you. This is nice," she said.

"Before you take a sip, there's one more thing we need to do."

"We do?"

"Yes." I couldn't wait any longer. I leaned toward her and brushed my lips against hers. Her lips parted, and I deepened the kiss. It was as delicious as I remembered, and long moments passed before I reluctantly ended our kiss. "I'd like to propose a toast."

"What are we toasting?" she asked.

"Seeing you again." I gently clinked my glass against hers.

A blush stained her cheeks pink, making her look more attractive than ever. "How about a toast to seeing each other again?"

I nodded. "I can do that."

During the ride to the restaurant, we talked about what had happened in our lives in the past few weeks. She was a dental hygienist for a thriving dental practice in Cambridge. I certainly admired her dedication and knew it was something I wouldn't want to do. Having my hands in other people's mouths did not appeal to me in the least. Probably the reason I'd never pursued a dental school education.

When we pulled up at the restaurant, Ellie's eyes widened in surprise. "Oh, I've never been to this Legal's before. It's perfect."

"Good. I'm glad." When the car stopped, I got out and offered my hand, helping her out. I was proud to have such a beautiful girl on my arm.

The first-floor restaurant was open to the fresh air and overlooked Boston Harbor. We walked to the hostess station.

"Reservation for Castian," I said.

"Of course. Please follow me."

It was a gorgeous day with a slight breeze blowing in off the water. Once at our table, I pulled out a chair for Ellie before taking a seat.

"Jess will be your waitress today," the hostess said. "She'll be right with you."

I nodded. "Thank you."

"What a perfect day to be here," Ellie said.

"I agree, but I think the company is what makes it perfect for me."

"You're so sweet," she said as she gave me a quick kiss.

The waitress came to our table before I had a chance to deepen the kiss.

"Welcome to Legal Harborside. My name is Jess, and I'll be taking care of you today. Can I get you something to drink?"

"Do you have lemonade?" Ellie asked.

Jess nodded. "And for you, sir?"

"I'll have soda water with lime."

"Very good. I'll be right back."

"Do you like lobster? I hear that's what this place is famous for." I said.

"Oh yes. I love lobster."

When Jess returned with our drinks, I ordered shrimp cocktail, Caesar salad, and steamed lobsters for us both. Throughout the meal, I could hardly keep my hands off Ellie. I had missed her more than I'd realized, and spending time with her again had rekindled my desire. It was certainly unusual for me. As a rule, I didn't warm up to people easily, but there was something so sweet and innocent about Ellie that she had managed to break down my walls effortlessly.

"Mmmm…this is so good," Ellie said between bites of lobster. "Thank you for picking this place."

"I'm glad you like it. You're right, this lobster is very good."

Jess came to clear the table. "Would you care for any coffee or dessert?"

I looked at Ellie, and she shook her head. "No, thanks. Just the check, please."

"Of course, right away."

The meal was a success, and we both left feeling full and satisfied.

"That was so good. Thank you for bringing me here," Ellie said.

I brought her hand to my lips for a gentle kiss. "The pleasure was all mine."

The car was waiting outside the entrance for us.

"Are you ready for your next surprise?" I asked.

Ellie giggled and rubbed her stomach. "Another one? I hope it doesn't involve food. I'm stuffed."

I pulled her close and kissed her. "No more food, I promise." I helped her into the car and slid in beside her. We were only in the car for fifteen minutes before it stopped again.

"You ready?" I asked.

"Absolutely."

I wanted to give Ellie a romantic afternoon, and there's nothing more romantic than a stroll through the Boston Public Gardens. It's a stunning oasis in the middle of a sea of steel and glass high-rise buildings. The garden's landscape exploded with a torrent of tulips in red, yellow, pink, and purple.

We walked hand in hand along the path, finally stopping on the bridge to admire the scenery. My arm slipped around her waist. She felt so good, and I wanted to hold her close. "Are you having a good time?"

She looked up at me and gave me a brilliant smile. "Oh, yes. I love the Gardens. It's actually one of my favorite places in town. How did you know?"

"I looked for the prettiest place in Boston to match the prettiest girl I've ever been with." I leaned down and gave her a tender kiss. "One more surprise. Come on." I took her hand and led her down to the loading area for the Swan Boats.

"The Swan Boats? Oh, Jared, you're so sweet," she said. "Thank you for planning such an extraordinary day."

"I'm glad you approve," I said as I took her hand and led her onto a Swan boat. I had enough tickets to go around the lake as many times as she wanted. The ride was magical, and I only had eyes for Ellie. She snuggled close to me and laid her head on my shoulder. I wrapped my arm around her waist and relished the feel of her. We ended up going around the lake five times before she grew tired of it.

"That was wonderful," she said as we walked back through the park. "I've had such a good time today."

"I have one more surprise for you."

"Really? Everything has been so wonderful. Believe me, there's no need for any more surprises."

The car was waiting outside the gates to Boston Gardens. We got in, and the driver drove us to the last stop of our date. "I thought we could finish our date with cocktails in the lounge at the Top of the Hub."

Ellie's eyes lit up. "Now you're really spoiling me."

"That's the plan."

We took the elevator to the lounge. Floor-to-ceiling windows gave patrons an expansive view of the city. Lights twinkled on and off in the various buildings of the downtown landscape. We were shown to a table, and I ordered a bottle of champagne. "Not sure if a jazz band is playing tonight, but I thought we could at least have a nightcap while admiring the Boston skyline."

"This is wonderful. I'm having such a good time."

"Shall I order us something to snack on with our drinks?"

She picked up one of the menus. "Want to split something sweet?"

"You mean something sweeter than you?"

She chuckled. "You're too much. Pick what you like. I'm sure I'll like whatever you choose."

"Sure." I gave our order to the waiter and turned my attention back to Ellie. "I'm so glad you agreed to come out with me. It's been a spectacular day, and I've enjoyed it immensely." I leaned closer, hoping for another searing kiss.

Chapter 7
Ellie

INHALED A SHARP BREATH WHEN Jared leaned toward me. I'd been waiting for him to kiss me again. It had been an absolutely spectacular day. No one had ever treated me like this on a date. I felt like a queen and couldn't get enough of his toe-curling kisses. His lips brushed mine before capturing my mouth completely as I welcomed his touch. The butterflies I'd had all day were in a frenzied dance with him so close. I've never had such an instant connection with anyone before. Was this real, or was I living in a fantasy world where the hero rides off into the sunset, never to be heard from again? My dating life before Jared had been unpleasant, to say the least, so I wasn't used to having such a great time.

The day had been perfect from the beginning. It was obvious Jared had put a lot of thought into our date, from my favorite food, to the romantic stroll around the Boston Gardens, to riding the Swan

Boats, to a nightcap at the Top of the Hub. I almost couldn't breathe for fear that, if I exhaled, it would all disappear, taking Jared with it.

When his lips touched mine, I let go of my insecurities and wild thoughts, and just enjoyed the moment. A thrill raced up my spine when his finger traced a line from my jaw to the hollow of my throat. How did this man know how to heat up my desire? It was as if I'd described the perfect man to a genie in the bottle, and then poof, there he was—handsome and sexy Jared, at your service. I wasn't going to question why the fates had brought him into my life. Instead, I let my senses take over as I became lost in the kiss. A fierce unexpected arousal nearly seared my bones. Goosebumps rose up on my arms as he deepened the kiss. Nothing else mattered as the noise fell away and Jared pulled me closer. I could feel the heat from his body and it stirred a deep longing in me. I had waited for someone like Jared for so long. Could he be the one I'd been looking for? I didn't know, but for now, I was going to enjoy being in his company.

I felt a deep sense of loss when he broke the kiss. I'd wanted it to go on forever.

"I'm not finished," he whispered in my ear as the waiter brought two flutes of champagne. He picked up his glass and said, "I want to thank you."

I raised my glass as well. "Thank me? For what?"

His glass lightly tapped mine. "For being you."

I couldn't help but smile. "Then I'll have to do the same," I said. "Today has been amazing, and it's even more special because I got to share it with you."

His smile made me feel like I was the only girl in the room, something I definitely could get used to. I gazed into Jared's beautiful blue eyes. I could drown in them; they were captivating.

The waiter brought dessert: a slice of Boston Cream pie. We took turns feeding forkfuls to each other. I'd always wanted to share desserts with someone, but the opportunity had never presented itself before today. The day had been perfection. I glanced at my watch, and while I hated to see the date end, I had to be realistic. "As much as I don't want this wonderful day to end, I have to work tomorrow."

"I know." Jared pulled out his phone and called the driver. "Yes, ten minutes. We'll be downstairs." He hung up and looked at me. "I totally understand and hope I haven't kept you out too late."

"Not at all. I've had a lovely time today. It was very special, but I have a full schedule tomorrow, beginning with a seven o'clock patient." A groan escaped my lips before I could stop it. It wasn't that I didn't enjoy my work, but sometimes I would love the opportunity to sleep in.

Jared signaled the waiter for the check, and soon we were downstairs in the Prudential Center lobby, waiting for the car. He took my hand, and the familiar warmth spread through me at his touch. Once inside the car, he put his arm around my shoulders, and my head came to rest on his shoulder. His fingers intertwined with mine, as we drove to my apartment. I'd never been happier.

When we reached my apartment building, he walked me to the door. Cupping my face in his hands, he gave me a kiss that scorched my insides and left me breathless.

"May I call you again?" he asked as he left a trail of kisses down my neck.

My mind was a whirlwind of emotions. I'd never felt such an intense connection with a man before. Was it a dream? Could I ever hope for anything more than this? I could hardly believe it, but his kisses were real, and a deep stirring pooling within me made me aware that I'd better stop kissing him now or I might do something I'd regret. I was not a girl who slept with a guy on the first date, however tempted I might be, and boy, did Jared tempt me.

I stepped out of his arms. "I would love that."

He gave me one last, sweet kiss that left me fumbling with my key. He waited until I had the door unlocked before he walked back to the car. He rolled down the window and waved one last time before the car disappeared into the night.

I don't remember what I did once I was inside my apartment because I was too busy reliving our perfect day together. When I finally crawled into bed, I hugged my pillow and daydreamed about Jared—his broad shoulders, his megawatt smile, those stunning blue eyes—the kind of eyes that draw you in and hold you there. I knew I'd be tired tomorrow, but when sleep finally found me, it was all worth it, as I relived Jared's kiss over and over.

I SHOULD HAVE KNOWN something that good wouldn't last. It had been three weeks since I saw Jared and I began to believe he had been simply too good to be true. I waited for him to call me, but for some reason, the call never came. As the days stretched into weeks, I began to doubt that Jared was ever going to call again. I'd thought we made a deep connection, but maybe I was wrong. What if that magical day had been nothing more than pure fantasy? How could he have touched me so deeply and then disappeared? Was that one perfect day all I would ever share with him?

I tried to banish such melancholy thoughts from my mind, but the glaring truth was that I hadn't heard from Jared in weeks. Not even a single text. Who doesn't have time for a text? I knew he was a busy lawyer, and maybe, just maybe, he really was over-extended at work and didn't have time to text. Back and forth conflicting thoughts continued to smash up against each other in my brain. One moment, I was devastated that he hadn't called me, and the next moment, I was giving him the benefit of the doubt. I hoped the latter was true because

Jared was a special guy, one that I wanted to get to know better. Time would tell if I ever got that chance.

After my last patient of the day, I cleaned up my area at the dental office and left the instruments out for the assistant to sterilize. Then I grabbed my bag and headed out for a dinner date with Danielle and Maggie. Maybe hanging out with my friends was what I needed to stop thinking about Jared. I hopped in my car and headed to Harvard Square. We'd agreed to try out a new place, Toscano. I wasn't sure I'd like the fancy dishes, but the menu featured both salads and pasta dishes. How can you go wrong with that?

It took me longer than expected to get through Harvard Square traffic, but I got lucky and grabbed a parking space on Brattle Street, not far from the restaurant. As soon as I walked into the restaurant, I was greeted with a smile from the hostess.

"Welcome to Toscano. Do you have a reservation?"

I looked around but didn't see either of my friends. "I'm meeting my friends. Has Danielle Peters or Maggie Hodges arrived yet?"

The young woman nodded. "Yes, they have. Let me show you to their table."

I followed her as she made her way around the tables. Rich, dark paneling and an exposed brick wall gave the place an Italian look. I found my friends sitting in the back corner by the brick wall. It was the perfect spot for a girl's night out full of laughing and gossip.

Danielle and Maggie were deep in conversation and didn't see me at first.

"I hope you're going to share that secret with me," I said as I pulled out a chair and joined them.

Danielle's eyes lit up. "You made it!"

"Yes. I even got a parking space on Brattle Street. How are you guys?"

The hostess slipped away, and a waiter came over to take my drink order.

"I'd like a glass of Chardonnay, please."

"Of course. I'll be right back with that." He looked at Danielle and Maggie. "Are you ladies all set, or would you like something else?"

Danielle spoke first. "I'm fine. Thank you."

Maggie echoed her.

When the waiter left, I leaned toward my friends. "So, what had you two so deep in conversation when I arrived?"

Maggie looked up, tears welling in her eyes.

I grabbed her hand. "Hey, what's the matter?"

"These are happy tears. I'm pregnant!"

"Wow, that's wonderful. I'm so happy for you. I didn't even know you guys were trying."

"We actually weren't, but when I took the test and it was positive, it turned out to be perfect timing."

The waiter brought my wine, and I lifted my glass. "To the best friends ever!" We tapped each other's glasses.

The food was outstanding, and the evening flew by as we caught up on gossip. Over dessert, Danielle asked the question I had been dreading all night. "So, what's up with you and Jared?"

I let out a pent-up sigh. "I wish I knew."

"Has he contacted you since the wedding?" Maggie asked.

I nodded. "Yes. He planned the most perfect date for us." I told my friends about that wonderful, magical day. Reliving it gave me a warm fuzzy feeling again, but it only served to remind me that I hadn't heard from him since that day.

"He must be busy," Danielle offered. "I'm sure, after putting that much effort into a date, that he's into you."

"I thought so, but—"

Danielle grabbed my hand. "No buts. You wait. He'll call again. I just know it."

"Well, I really don't have any choice in the matter. I did send him a thank-you text after our date, but I haven't heard back from him." I said with a forced chuckle. I was not going to spoil my time with my friends by stressing over whether or not Jared would call me again. "We'll see if he contacts me again, although I'm not holding my breath. If he never calls again, I can at least say we had one perfect date. That's better than any of my other dates lately."

After an enjoyable night of excellent food, wine, and conversation with my friends, I got in my car for the drive home. Was Danielle right? Would Jared call again? I wanted to be optimistic, but that nagging little demon on my shoulder continued to shake my confidence.

If he was into you, he would have called by now. Give it up. He's done with you.

As I was putting my key in my apartment door, my phone dinged. I dug around in my purse and pulled out my phone, thinking it was Danielle, checking to make sure I got home okay. I smiled when I read the text.

I'M THINKING ABOUT YOU.

My heart did a little pitter-patter. Danielle had been right after all. The proof was in Jared's text. I thought about my answer before sending it. I didn't want to assume anything, but I wanted him to know I was thinking about him as well. Maybe that was all I needed to say.

I'M THINKING OF YOU AS WELL.

I held my breath, waiting to see if another text would come in. It was unlike me to get so wrapped up in a guy I had just met. My dating history had taught me that much at least. I was a more reserved type of girl, waiting to see how things progressed before I engaged my heart, but Jared had shattered all my attempts at staying aloof with one perfect date. Should I continue to trust my heart, or was I a bigger fool than I realized?

I walked into my apartment and threw my purse and keys on the kitchen counter before I poured a glass of wine. Might as well be comfortably stretched out on my couch while I waited. As the minutes ticked by, my stomach clenched and I could hardly breathe. Was that all he was going to say?

I hated the fact that he could fluster me with a single text. I had been getting used to the fact that I'd never see him again, and then his sweet text comes in. Now what? Was he going to string me along for another three weeks?

Chapter 8
Jared

CRINGED WHEN I REALIZED THAT it had been almost three weeks since I last saw Ellie. I hadn't even had time to send her a text. She must think I was blowing her off, but the truth was, this merger business was more complicated and time-consuming than I had originally thought. Non-stop meetings in fifteen-hour days had taken up all my time. More prepping at night meant I didn't have a minute to spare before I fell exhausted into bed for a few hours sleep.

Determined not to let another day go by before contacting her, I reached for my phone. I wanted to test the waters with a text first. If she didn't respond, I'd take the hint that our one date was also our last date. I hoped I hadn't blown my chances with her, because I had enjoyed myself immensely that day. She was everything I could hope for—beautiful, fun, sassy, and yet, there was something else that had thoroughly captured my attention. Her kisses filled me a burning desire that I hadn't felt in a long time, and I wanted more, a lot more.

When my phone dinged and I read her text, I knew I had to make plans to see her again. I remembered she'd said that she loved watching the Boston Red Sox. Her dad had taken her and her two brothers to the games when they were kids, but she hadn't been to a game in years. I made a few phone calls and snagged two tickets along the first base line. I would owe Bill a steak dinner, but it was worth it to get the tickets.

I texted Ellie. YOU FREE SATURDAY?

Her reply came immediately. YES. WHAT DO YOU HAVE IN MIND?

SOMETHING SPECIAL. CASUAL WEAR. I hoped that would be clear enough. It didn't matter to me what she wore—she looked great in everything—but I wanted her to be comfortable at the game.

SOUNDS FUN. WHAT TIME?

I'LL PICK YOU UP AT ELEVEN.

CAN'T WAIT. HAVE A GOOD WEEK.

Have a good week—I didn't know what that was anymore. I'd been grinding away since graduating law school, crawling my way up the corporate ladder of the third most prestigious law firm in Washington, D.C. That didn't leave much time for a social life. Until I met Ellie, my dating life had consisted of a few dates with fellow lawyers. But who wanted to talk shop all the time? I'd found it better not to date at all.

When one of the senior partners told me they were transferring me to Boston to oversee the merger of two of our biggest clients, I'd groaned inwardly. But now, the move had introduced me to the best thing that had happened to me in years, and her name was Ellie Davidson.

Funny, I'd never thought I believed in the whole concept of love at first sight. Was it possible to fall for someone you'd just met? Yes. I believed it was, and I wanted Ellie to feel special. She already held a special place in my heart. Now I had to wait three more days before I could show her how special she was becoming to me. It was going to be a long week.

By the time Saturday morning rolled around, I was chomping at the bit to see her. My eyes popped open at six in the morning—so much for sleeping in. I got up, enjoyed a cup of coffee, and then went for a run on Boston Common. At that time of the morning, there wasn't anyone around except other avid runners. As we passed, we gave each other slight nods. Only fitness fanatics and nervous boyfriends were out running this early.

Boyfriend.

Did I just think boyfriend? Is that what I want to be?

As soon as I thought of Ellie's expressive eyes, rich brown curls, and those sweet lips, I knew that was indeed what I wanted to be—Ellie's boyfriend.

I ran for an hour, hopped in a hot shower, and enjoyed a leisurely breakfast of eggs and bacon. There was still time for me to get a little work done before the car came around downstairs. The more I did on this complicated merger now, the less I'd have to do tomorrow.

Thirty minutes later, my phone dinged with a text from the driver. Finally time to see Ellie. I closed down my laptop and grabbed my apartment keys before heading outside. The roads to Ellie's apartment in Somerville were clogged with traffic. Everyone and their brother were out doing errands. When we finally arrived at Ellie's place, I jumped out of the car. Much to my surprise, Ellie was already exiting her front door.

"Hi Jared," she said with a wave.

She looked stunning in white jeans and a navy blue top. Her hair was pulled back in a ponytail, showing off her high cheekbones to perfection. She looked radiant. I pulled her into my arms and kissed her, long and deep. "Hi, yourself," I said when we broke apart.

"That's quite a hello," she said with a chuckle. "I like it."

"I aim to please," I said with a gleam of devilry in my eyes. "Shall we go?"

She nodded and slipped her arm through mine. I opened the car door, and she scooted inside.

"I do have a car, you know. I can pick you up sometime."

"I'm not worried about that. Where we're going, it might be difficult to find a parking space. As long as I have a car at my disposal, might as well use it, right?"

"I guess so."

The look of wonder on her face when we pulled up to Fenway Park was priceless.

"Oh my god! I can't believe you got tickets for today's game against the Yankees."

"I remembered you said you loved it when your dad took you and your brothers to the game. I thought it would be a fun way to spend some time together."

"Yes, absolutely! It's perfect."

We had front row seats to the action along the third base line.

"These are such great seats," Ellie said. "How did you get them?"

"A friend of mine came through for me. I'll owe him a steak dinner, but it's so worth it."

"Please give him my thanks as well."

At the sound of the bat hitting a foul ball, our attention became riveted on home plate. Batter after batter came up as the afternoon flew by. It was a close game, tied at four apiece through seven innings. In the top of the eighth inning, the Yankees went three batters up, three batters down. Before the Red Sox came up to bat, "Sweet Caroline" by Neil Diamond came over the loud speakers, and the crowd went wild.

Ellie started singing, and I looked around our section. Everyone was standing up and singing. I'd never seen such a display of sheer joy.

"Come on, you have to sing. It's tradition," Ellie said, pulling me to my feet.

I didn't know the words, but by the second chorus, I was singing right along with everyone else. It was the most fun I'd ever had a baseball game, and the joy on Ellie's face was priceless.

At the bottom of the eighth inning, two outs, it was Big Papi's turn at the plate. One batter had made it to first base, and Ortiz was the closer. Could he pull off another epic at bat? I watched as he stared down the pitcher. The count was three-two, and the crowd held their breath. The runner on first base was edging off the bag, waiting for a chance to steal. The pitcher wound up and delivered a blazing fastball right into the path of Ortiz's bat. The crack of the bat hitting the ball had the crowd on their feet as they watched the ball soar over the Green Monster. As Ortiz rounded the bases, the roar of the crowd was infectious. I was screaming his name along with everyone else.

Ellie was squeezing my arm. "Did you see that? What a shot," she said. "It just sailed over the wall. Unbelievable!"

The Red Sox won the game six to four, and I thoroughly enjoyed myself. The biggest reason was having Ellie by my side. The more time I spent with her, the more I wanted to see her. I couldn't wait for this merger to be completed so I'd have more time to spend with her. I hoped she would understand the situation and wouldn't think I was stringing her along, because that was the furthest thing from my mind.

On the ride back to Ellie's apartment, I squeezed her hand. "I had such a good time today. I'm sorry it's been so long between dates, but this merger is taking more time than I'd originally thought."

Ellie leaned her head on my shoulder. "I understand. I'm just glad we had today together. It was perfect."

"Yes, it was." I tilted her chin up and tasted her sweet lips. They were soft, and I couldn't get enough of her. She parted her lips, and I deepened the kiss. My hand caressed her cheek, and a soft moan escaped her. I was falling hard for this girl. It was the first time in quite a while that someone had piqued my interest and it made me realize I was in this relationship for the long haul.

Over the next several months, I tried hard to make sure I was free on Saturday nights so Ellie and I could spend them together. The more time I spent in her company, the more I wanted. I knew some people would think it was too soon for me to have such feelings for Ellie, but sometimes, you just know when it's right. Ellie was the right girl for me. I knew it deep in my bones, and I wasn't about to let my schedule or this merger ruin my chance to be with her.

One evening in December, as I was seeing her home after another lovely night, I asked, "So, are you free next Saturday night?"

"Yes. Are you asking me for another date?" she asked with a sly smile.

I leaned in and kissed her. "You know I am. Any place in particular you'd like to go next week?"

"I have an idea."

"What?"

"You've mentioned that you like Italian food?

I nodded. "Love it. Why? Is there someplace you'd like to go?"

She shook her head. "No. I want to cook for you. I make a mean lasagna."

"Sounds great. What time do you want me to be at your place?" I asked.

"How's six?"

"Perfect." I couldn't resist and pulled her close for another kiss. After several searing kisses, I reluctantly let her go. "Until next week."

I opened the car door, helped her out, and waited until she was inside her apartment before we drove off.

Another hell week with the merger kept me busy every night. I was thrilled that it would finally be over by next week. The client was scheduled to travel to the Washington office and sign the final papers on Monday morning. By the time I crawled into bed

Friday night, all I could think of was Ellie and my plan to make her mine.

Saturday morning rolled around, and I woke up feeling nervous. I had a couple of errands to do that day before I headed to Ellie's place for dinner. I glanced at my watch. Time to go. The driver had texted me that he was downstairs waiting, so I grabbed my coat and headed out.

"Good morning, sir," the driver said.

"Morning, Tom. I'd like to go to Tiffany's at Copley Place."

Tom nodded and pulled out into traffic.

I wasn't sure exactly when it had happened, but I knew that Ellie was the woman of my dreams and I loved her more than words could express. Tonight, I was going to ask her to marry me, but first, I had to find the perfect diamond. She deserved the best, and I was determined to find a ring that suited her.

A young woman greeted me when I walked into Tiffany's. "Good morning, sir. May I help you with something?"

I nodded. "Yes. I'm looking for an engagement ring."

"Of course. I can help you with that. Please join me at the counter to your right."

After looking at numerous rings, I settled on the Soleste Heart style with a center diamond of two carats surrounded by smaller diamonds. The ring was flawless, just like Ellie, and I could hardly wait to see her face tonight when I proposed. After taking care of the payment, I slipped the distinctive blue box in my pocket before heading off to the Armani Exchange store. I wanted to look my best tonight. I enjoyed a leisurely lunch at the mall before returning to the car. I had time for a shower and shave before heading to Ellie's place for dinner. It was time to put Operation Ellie into play.

Tom was downstairs waiting, and I slipped into the back seat.

"Any more errands, sir?"

"No. I'm finished. Let's head back to the apartment."

Tom nodded. "Very good."

I fingered the box in my pocket as we drove back to the apartment. I had never felt so contented before. Ellie was like a bright star shining down on me, filling me with the most incredible feelings. I loved her with every fiber of my being and I wanted to spend every day and night with her. Tonight, I hoped that Ellie would make me a very happy man.

Chapter 9
Ellie

I COULDN'T STOP SMILING. MY LIFE was perfect. The summer and autumn months had flown by, and Jared and I were still together basking in the glow of each other's company. Saturday had become our time together. We enjoyed going to the movies, spending time with Steve and Danielle, and quiet dinners just for us. I had even brought him along to Thanksgiving dinner with my family, and he'd charmed my mother and gotten along well with my father and brothers. All he'd had to say was that he was a fan of Tom Brady and the Patriots, and he was one of them. That was a huge relief for me. It was one more hurdle in our courtship that had gone flawlessly so far.

Jared was everything I could have asked for in a man, and I was falling in love with him. For the first time in my life, I knew what an all-consuming love felt like, and it was glorious. His smile sent my insides quivering, and his kisses consumed me.

Tonight, I was preparing a special dinner for him. It was a big night for me because I planned to tell Jared I loved him and seduce him into my bed. While we enjoyed each other's company immensely, neither of us had spoken those three special words. I didn't mind being the first; after all, I had kissed him first when our journey together began, and it just seemed right.

I grabbed my coat, wrapped my scarf around my head and face, and braved the cold wind on my way to the grocery store. December had indeed roared in like some ravenous ice beast whose only instinct was to freeze every inch of exposed skin. I didn't want to go out, but I needed some ingredients for our dinner. Tonight, I was making lasagna with meat sauce. Jared had mentioned he liked Italian food, and I wanted the night to be perfect.

Ninety minutes later, I lugged the grocery bags back to my apartment. I had also bought a bouquet of flowers to grace the table and a bottle of wine. It was eleven o'clock in the morning, and Jared would be here at six. I had time to clean, cook, and take a shower.

The hours slipped by as I hummed a happy tune, and by five o'clock, I had finished with everything. The lasagna was in the oven, the sauce was simmering, the table had been set with flowers and candles, and I'd opened the wine to breathe. All that was left was for me to take a shower. I stepped into the shower and let the hot water wash away the tension in my shoulders. I was nervous about tonight, even though I was committed to telling Jared how I felt about him. I would offer her everything? Would he welcome it? I was sure he'd enjoy the sex part, although he had never pushed me for sex. I knew my desire was always raging after one of our make-out sessions, so I imagined his was as well. Still, I worried. Some guys were commitment-phobic, but that didn't seem to fit Jared's behavior over the past seven months. If anything, he seemed even more attentive and loving as time went on. I'd begun to believe I could have my own happily ever after, like my college friends had found. Me, little five-foot-two Ellie with the unmanageable curly hair, had found the man of her dreams. A delightful shiver raced up my spine as I thought about Jared's kisses.

By the time I finished my shower, blew dry my hair, and reapplied my makeup, it was nearly six. I didn't want my intentions for later this evening to be too obvious, so I dressed in a cranberry cashmere sweater and black wool slacks before heading out to the kitchen to check on dinner.

He would be here any minute. Jared had never been late for one of our dates, and I could hardly contain my excitement. It was going to be a life-changing night, at least for me. I'd never told anyone that I loved them before. It had taken a very special man to capture my heart, and Jared was that man.

Chapter 10
Jared

*T*OM TEXTED ME THAT HE was downstairs, and I picked up the blue box and put it in my jacket pocket. I didn't want Ellie to see it until I was ready to propose. I had thought about what I would say to her besides "will you marry me." I wanted to tell her she was the most special girl in the world to me and when she came into my life, she'd brought laughter and sunshine into it. I'd been too driven at work to see what I was missing out on. Someone warm and loving waiting at home for you, giving you that perfect smile to make your troubles go away; a special someone who made your world whole. That was what I wanted to tell her.

"Where to tonight, sir?" Tom asked.

I'd opened my mouth to tell him Ellie's place when my phone rang. I pulled it out of my pocket and looked at the caller ID. It was one of the senior partners from Washington. I found it odd that he'd be calling me on a

Saturday evening and was tempted to ignore the call, but whatever they wanted would only be waiting for me later. It was better to deal with it now.

"Castian."

"Jared, I'm glad I caught you. We need you back in Washington immediately."

"Mark, what's going on?"

"The merger is falling apart. We need you to smooth the deal with the client. He respects your opinion and has said that he'll only continue if you're the lawyer in the room."

I swore silently. I had worked on that merger for months, making sure all the i's were dotted and the t's were crossed. I couldn't believe there could be a problem at this late stage. "Did Mike say that specifically?"

"Yes. My secretary emailed the boarding pass for the six-thirty shuttle. We're having dinner with Mike tonight, and with you there, this merger will have a chance of going through."

I shook my head not quite believing what had happened with Mike. Everything had been set yesterday. What could have possibly happened in a day? This was not how I had planned for this evening to play out. Getting called back to Washington was the worst possible timing, but I couldn't ignore the client at this stage. "I'll be there," I said and hung up. I took a moment to fume about the unfairness of this situation. I had been looking forward to spending the evening with Ellie. I had made sure to clear everything yesterday so nothing could interfere with our date. So much for trying to be organized.

"Tom, I need to go back up to the apartment and pack a bag and then go to Logan."

"Of course, sir."

I barely had enough time to pack before my boss called again. He talked throughout the ride to Logan about the particulars he wanted brought up at dinner. I made it through security at Logan in time for my flight. I raced to my gate and got there in the nick of time, just before they closed the door. Once in my seat, I pulled out my phone. I had to tell Ellie what was going on. She was expecting me at her place half an hour ago. I hated to disappoint her, but once this deal was done, my life would get a lot easier, which meant I could spend more time with her. I started texting her.

The stewardess leaned toward me and said, "Sir, you'll need to shut your phone off or put it in airplane mode. We're backing away from the gate."

I nodded and sent what I had managed to type hoping that she would understand the reason for me bailing on our date. I was still fuming about the timing, but I wanted this merger over with so I could propose to Ellie. She was the woman of my dreams, and I wanted to spend the rest of my life with her. Damn the timing of this trip.

Chapter 11
Ellie

EVERYTHING LOOKED GOOD, AND THE smell permeating the apartment was mouth-watering. I hoped the food tasted as good as it smelled. I'd made lasagna many times before; I just hoped this time nothing would go wrong. My phone was sitting on the kitchen counter, and I saw there was a text from Jared and was curious to see what it said. Jared had never been late for our dates and I could hardly wait for him to get here. I picked up the phone and read the text.

SORRY. I CAN'T.

What? What did that mean—I can't come to dinner or I can't see you anymore? I kept waiting for another text to come in and explain what he meant, but there was nothing but silence. There had to be an explanation for this, I thought, trying to avoid the awful truth staring me in the face. Had he somehow figured out what I was going to say to him tonight? Was he one of those commitment-phobic guys after all? How could that be? His actions over the past several months told me a different story.

But maybe it was I who hadn't read the situation correctly. His text could only mean one thing, and the breath fled my body as I doubled over. I felt like I'd been hit with a sledgehammer. Misery spread through my heart. He was breaking up with me. I tried to think of something else the text could mean, but I quickly lost that battle. I should have known better than to think our relationship would progress to the next level. My insecurity reared its ugly head.

He's done with it. You didn't measure up.

He clearly didn't feel the same about me as I felt about him if he was breaking up with me via a text message. Who does that? He was such a coward. It was painfully obvious he didn't want a messy break-up scene. I crumpled to the floor, holding the phone, staring at the words through my tears. I should have protected my heart better. Now it was too late. Great sobs wracked my body. He didn't want me anymore. Even though the proof was in his text, I didn't want to believe it. How could it be? His every touch and kiss had told me such a different story. The pain of realizing that he no longer wanted me in his life left me bereft, and I gave in to my sorrow, sobbing uncontrollably on the kitchen floor.

I don't know how long I stayed there crying. I had to let the pain out and couldn't think beyond the betrayal.

I came back to myself when I heard the oven ding. The lasagna was ready. It was seven o'clock.

I dragged myself off the floor and went to the stove, pulling the lasagna out and shutting off the gas under the sauce. I'd have to let the food cool down before I could put it in the fridge.

My phone was still on the floor, where I had held it, hoping against hope that the text from Jared didn't mean what I thought it meant. I picked it up and put it back on the counter before pouring myself a glass of wine and plopping down on the couch. I knew I shouldn't torture myself with "what ifs," but I couldn't help it. I relived all our wonderful dates together, trying to find something that could have prepared me for this. I didn't understand. How could he throw away everything we had shared together?

My first instinct had been to call Danielle and tell her what happened, but the pain was too raw. I knew I wouldn't get two words out before the tears began again. It would be better if I let some time pass before I told anyone, although who was I kidding? It would take a very long time, if ever, for me to recover from this heartache. I was in too deep and had given Jared every piece of my heart. I had not protected even a little sliver of it and now I was paying the price. Devastation licked through me and became a white-hot fury. I couldn't breathe and the tears continued to flow.

Chapter 12
Jared

OR THE NEXT DAY AND a half, I was with our client, explaining every aspect of the merger. I'd already done this in Boston, but Mike was uncomfortable until I was there with him in Washington. When the deal was finally done, I was beyond relieved that I could now get back to Ellie. I planned to take the early morning shuttle back to Boston. I couldn't wait to see my girl again, soon to be my wife, if everything went according to plan.

That night at the hotel, I called Ellie. I was looking forward to hearing her voice, but the call went straight to voicemail. That was odd. I wondered if she was out with friends and didn't hear the phone ring. The same scenario played out when I tried to call her in the morning, and then again when I landed back in Boston. What was going on? Why was she refusing to accept my calls?

When I finally looked back at my last text to her, I was appalled at my own stupidity. I should have taken the time to finish the text. No wonder she was refusing my calls. I stared at the text.

SORRY. I CAN'T.

It sounded like I was breaking up with her. No wonder she wasn't taking my calls. What a blazing idiot I was. I should have explained what was happening right away, but the damage was done. The question now was—could I undo it? I hoped so, but I needed help fixing this situation.

I scrolled through my contacts until I found the right number and hit the call button.

"Hey, Jared. What's up?" Steve said.

"Listen, man. I screwed up, and I need help fixing this."

"Wow, that's something new for you. What happened?"

"Leave it to me to foul things up. This is bad. Really bad." I explained the situation to him. "I need the Davidsons' phone number."

"You're right. That's pretty bad."

"Will you help me fix it?"

"Of course. I'll text you the Davidsons' number."

By the time I hung up with Steve, we had a plan. It was time to get Ellie back. I couldn't lose the woman I loved. She was my heart and soul, my absolute everything. She was the reason I woke up in the morning. I couldn't imagine my life without her. I called her parents and explained what had happened. Even with them on board, I had to wait until Saturday to fix my blunder. I didn't even want to think about the fact that Ellie might refuse me.

The next four days crawled by. I didn't try to call Ellie again. I was pinning all my hopes on this plan. I arrived at her parents' house for their annual Christmas Eve party an hour before Ellie was due to arrive.

"Jared, come in," Mrs. Davidson said.

"Thanks, Mrs. Davidson. Do you have enough vases?" I asked, putting six dozen red roses on the counter.

"Yes," she said, pointing to the vases behind her. "The candles are all set up in the family room as well, plus the mistletoe is hung just where you asked."

I gave her a hug. "Thank you for everything. You can't imagine how sorry I am about this misunderstanding. I want Ellie to know what she means to me. I never meant to hurt her. You must believe me on that."

Mrs. Davidson nodded. "I know. Misunderstandings happen in love, but it will all work out. I know my Ellie."

Steve and Danielle arrived a few moments behind me. "Nice touch," Steve said, looking at the roses.

I shook Steve's hand and kissed Danielle on the cheek. "Thanks for helping me set this up."

Danielle nodded. "Wouldn't miss this for the world. I've been to the Davidsons' Christmas Eve party more times than I can count, but this one will be extra special. I can't wait to see Ellie's face when you propose."

"I just hope she forgives me."

"Have faith, Jared. She'll come around."

Danielle and Mrs. Davidson began cutting the stems of the roses and putting them in water.

Finally, the roses were scattered around the family room, the Christmas tree lights were on, the candles were lit, and the mistletoe was hung from the ceiling by the tree. This was where I would ask the woman I loved to marry me. I wanted everything to be perfect. It better work because I didn't have a Plan B. Now I needed to wait for Ellie to arrive. Luckily, I didn't have to wait overly long. Otherwise, I might have worn a hole in the carpet, pacing back and forth in front of the tree.

I heard her greet her family, Steve and Danielle, and then her mother asked her to take a present into the family room and put it under the tree. I took my place in front of the Christmas tree and waited. I was scarcely breathing, and my heart pounded in my chest in anticipation. I'd never been so nervous before. This was the moment I'd been waiting for—my chance to let Ellie know what she means to me. My beautiful sweet Ellie was everything I wanted.

I watched her expression of wonder as she walked into the room and looked around at all the roses. It took her a moment to see me standing there.

The smile immediately left her face. "Jared, what are you doing here?"

I plunged ahead, not letting her say anything more. "Ellie, will you come and stand with me?"

She hesitated. "I don't think that's a good idea."

Her mother came up behind her and whispered something in her ear. Ellie waited a moment longer before she walked to me. Everyone else crowded in the doorway.

I felt a bead of sweat roll down my back. I wanted to make this right and took hold of her hand. "Ellie, I was an idiot for sending you such a hurried text. It didn't mean what you thought."

She pulled her hand away. "Really? Because it was pretty clear to me that you were breaking up with me. I've had a week to think about all this, and it's probably a good thing you're here because now I can tell you to your face. We're done."

"Will you please listen to me for a moment?" I pleaded.

"I don't understand why you're in my parent's house. This party is for family and friends, and right now, you are neither of those things."

I shook my head vigorously. "Just let me explain, please? Grant me five minutes of your time."

"Five minutes, and then I want you gone."

I nodded knowing I had to talk fast. "I got a call from my firm when I was on my way to your house last Saturday. They needed me in Washington right away to basically hold hands with the client in that big merger

I've been working on. I barely made the flight and was texting you as we pushed back from the gate. The flight attendant was adamant that I had to shut off the phone. I hurriedly sent the text and put the phone on airplane mode. I thought I had written more of an explanation about why I wouldn't be there for dinner. The client kept me so busy, it was almost two days before I had a moment to call you."

Ellie's face was unreadable. For the first time since I met her, I didn't know what she was thinking.

"I'm so sorry for the hurt I've caused you and hope that you can forgive me."

She turned to go. "Jared, you need to leave now. I'm not playing these games with you anymore. All warm and fuzzy one moment and cold and heartless the next. I don't need it, and I'm done with all that."

I reached out and grabbed her arm. "Please don't go. There's more." I pulled the blue box out of my pocket. "Ellie Davidson, this is what I wanted to do Saturday night." I opened the box and knelt in front of her. "You're the most important person in my life. I'm not playing any games. I promise you that. Your smile lights up a room, your laugh makes me happy, and your sweet kisses mean everything to me. You have captured my heart and soul, and I love you with every fiber of my being."

Ellie stared at the box. "You do?"

"Yes. I do, and I don't want to spend another day without you." I opened the box and pulled out the ring. "Would you do me the great honor of becoming my wife?"

Ellie's mouth fell open as she stared at the diamond. It took her a moment to recover her voice. "I don't know what to say. I'd hardened my heart against you and now you're here proposing." Tears spilled down her cheeks. "I thought you didn't want me. This past week has been the most horrible week of my life. The world turned gray, and I felt devoid of all happiness. I didn't know how I could face life without you. But now, you're here telling me everything that I had hoped to tell you last week. Saturday, I was going to tell you I loved you over dinner."

I smiled. "Does that mean you accept my proposal?"

She swiped the tears from her cheeks and rewarded me with the prettiest smile I'd ever seen. "Yes. On one condition."

"Anything, my love."

"From now on I want a phone call if something comes up. No more texting."

"You got it. I've learned my lesson." I took her left hand and slid the ring on her finger.

"Oh my god, it's beautiful," she said before throwing herself into my arms. "I love you so much."

I pulled her close and kissed her under the mistletoe. I'd won the heart of the woman of my dreams, and I couldn't have been happier.

Her mother and Danielle were the first people through the door. They were hugging and crying.

Steve slapped me on the back. "Welcome to the land of the married." He leaned closer to whisper in my ear. "It will be the best time of your life, but don't let the ladies hear you say that too often."

I chuckled and gazed upon my beautiful Ellie. "I don't mind telling her that every day, twice a day, if that's what she wants."

Chapter 13
Ellie

THE MOMENT I SAW JARED standing next to the Christmas tree, my heart thudded in my chest and my breath left me. Why was he here? He looked impossibly handsome, and against my better judgment, the usual thrill at seeing him raced up my spine. How could I be happy to see him when a week ago, he'd sent me a break-up text? Should I turn around and leave? I might have if it hadn't been my parents' party. It was too late at that point to do anything except take a deep breath and steel myself for whatever happened next.

I knew I might as well give Jared a chance to explain before I walked away from him. I needed closure for our ill-fated love affair, and he was the only one who could give me the answers I craved. As I listened to him explain what had happened last Saturday night, the ice that had formed around my heart began to crack. The last thing I expected when I walked into my parents' home for their

239

annual Christmas Eve party was to leave engaged to the man of my dreams. I was floating on air, and later, I didn't remember much about the rest of the night besides Jared kissing me under the mistletoe. I'm sure I smiled every time he pulled me under it. I could have stayed there all night, kissing him.

The next day, we were invited to Danielle and Steve's for Christmas brunch. I had offered to make a ham and cheese quiche, and it was almost done when I heard the doorbell ring. Jared was right on time.

I opened the door and was surprised when I saw his arms full of presents. "What's all this?" I asked.

He gave me a slow and sexy smile that made me weak in the knees. I was still in shock that this hunky guy was all mine.

"Just a few things I picked up for my wife-to-be," he said as he put the gifts down under my little three-foot Christmas tree.

"But I don't have anything for you," I complained.

"Not necessary," he said, and once his arms were free, he pulled me close and kissed me long and deep.

"Mmmmm…I could get used to that," I said.

"Promise?" he asked.

I gazed into his beautiful eyes and nodded. "For the rest of my life." He kissed me again until the oven dinged, interrupting us. I reluctantly stepped out of his arms. "Quiche is done. We really should get going."

"Okay, but I hope we aren't staying too long. I want to Skype with my parents and tell them the good news."

"You think your parents will be happy?" I was feeling nervous about announcing our engagement to them when I hadn't even met them yet.

"They'll be thrilled, trust me. I've been getting subtle hints for a few years now. I supposed they figured I should be married, especially since two of my younger brothers are already married."

"Let's get going then," I said. I went into the kitchen, took the quiche out of the oven, and put it into an insulated bag.

"Here, let me carry that," Jared said as he picked up the bag.

It didn't take long to get to our friends' house. "Merry Christmas," I said, hugging Danielle when she opened the door.

"Come in, come in," she said.

"Quiche is still hot," Jared said.

"Awesome. Everything is ready. Come into the dining room and let's eat."

"Good. I'm starving," Steve said.

The table was overflowing with food. "Wow, everything looks fantastic," I said.

"You guys want coffee?" Danielle asked.

Jared and I nodded. "Yes," we said in unison.

Once we all started eating, Danielle asked, "So, have you guys set a date yet?"

I looked at Jared. "We haven't talked about it yet, but I for one don't want a long engagement."

That brought a smile to Jared's face. "How about February?" he asked.

"You want us to plan a wedding in two months?" Danielle asked.

"I don't want a big wedding," I said. "Just family and close friends will be fine with me."

Jared agreed. "We're talking to my parents later today, so we'll see if they'll be able to come out here in February."

"Well, let me know what I can do to help," Danielle said. "I'll round up the girls. Any idea what you want us to wear?"

I chuckled. "Definitely not chiffon dresses. I was thinking of cranberry as the accent color. I don't really care what style of dress you all wear, as long as they're all the same color. I definitely want dresses that you can wear again."

"Once you agree on a date, let me know, and I'll get going on the dresses, okay?" Danielle asked.

"That would be awesome," I said, grateful that I didn't have to go to endless appointments, searching for bridesmaid dresses. "I also want to try to get something off the rack for my dress. We could go to David's Bridal. I'm sure something will appeal to me."

"Just name the day, and I'll be there," Danielle said.

After spending two hours with Danielle and Steve, we headed back to my apartment. I was excited and nervous. What if his parents didn't like me? Would Jared still want to marry me? I knew that he was close with his family, and I didn't want to be the one to cause any tension.

"Do you want a drink before we Skype with your parents?" I asked.

Jared nodded. "Let's open the champagne so we can have a toast with them. How does that sound?"

I hesitated, and Jared furrowed his brows.

"What's wrong," he asked, pulling into his arms.

"What if they don't like me?" I asked.

He leaned down and gave me a sweet, tender kiss. "Trust me. They'll love you."

He went into the kitchen, popped open the champagne, and poured two flutes. "Are you ready?" he asked as he put the flutes on the coffee table.

I nodded and turned on my laptop.

His parents were already online, and I clicked on the video button. It didn't take them long to answer.

"Merry Christmas," Jared said.

"Merry Christmas," his mom said before his dad chimed in.

Before I had a chance to wish them a Merry Christmas, Jared held up my left hand. "Surprise! I'm engaged. This is Ellie Davidson, the love of my life."

"Merry Christmas, Mr. and Mrs. Castian," I said.

His mother's eyes widened in surprise. "Engaged?"

Jared nodded. We could hear his dad over to the computer saying, "Your brother is engaged."

Two more handsome faces loomed into the picture.

Jared pointed to the screen. "Austin and Derek, my younger brothers," he said.

"It's about time," Austin said. "Hi Ellie, nice to meet you."

"It's wonderful to meet you all," I said.

"Have you set a date yet?" Mrs. Castian asked.

Jared nodded. "We were thinking some time in February. Can you guys make that work?"

"We have no plans at the moment, so pick a date and we'll be there," she said.

I picked up my phone and scrolled to February. "What about February 21?"

Jared's family each looked through their own phones. Everyone nodded. "That works perfectly," Mrs. Castian said.

"Fantastic," Jared said. "As soon as we figure out the details, I'll let you know."

By the time we hung up with his family, I was flushed, either from their excitement about the engagement or the champagne, maybe both.

Jared pulled me into his arms. "See, what did I tell you? I knew they'd love you."

"I'm so glad. I certainly didn't want to cause any problems with your family."

He caressed my cheek. "You are perfect, my beautiful sweet girl. Everyone who knows you loves you, but no one will ever love you more than I do. I bless the day I was transferred to Boston."

I leaned in and kissed him. "You are perfect for me as well, and you've made so very happy."

The next two months flew by. We chose to have the ceremony at a little stone chapel on the grounds of Tufts University and had booked a private room at the Four Seasons Hotel for lunch after the ceremony.

I stood at the back of the chapel with my college friends. They'd all come through and looked beautiful in knee-length cranberry velvet dresses. "You guys look beautiful," I said.

"And you outshine us all," Danielle said. "You're one of the prettiest brides I've ever seen. Wait until Jared sees you."

I did feel beautiful and, for the first time since I'd meet them, not overshadowed by my friends. "Thank you. I'm so happy you're all here."

"We wouldn't miss it for the world," Meghan chimed in.

My dad walked to my side. "Are you ready, sweetheart?"

I nodded. "Never been more ready in my life."

He smiled. "Well, let's get this show on the road then."

The bridal party lined up and were soon walking down the aisle. I followed on my dad's arm, smiling at the guests as we made our way to the front of the chapel.

Jared stood tall next to his brothers. He had tears in his eyes. "You look beautiful," he whispered as my dad and I came to stand next to him.

The Justice of the Peace welcomed everyone. "Who gives this woman to this man?" he asked.

"Her mother and I do," my dad said. He lifted my veil and kissed my cheek before placing my right hand in Jared's.

The ceremony wasn't overly long. Austin did a reading, and we had a violin soloist play while we lit the unity candle. We gave our mothers each a long-stemmed red rose, and then those magical words we had been waiting for were finally here.

"I now pronounce you husband and wife," the Justice of the Peace said. "Jared, you may kiss your beautiful bride."

Our first kiss as a married couple was perfect. Jared dipped me and kissed me, a kiss that told me how much he loved me. Life couldn't get any better than this.

After the kiss, we turned toward our guests. "We did it," Jared shouted to applause.

I was overjoyed and couldn't keep the smile from my face. I had married the man of my dreams, and I couldn't wait to see what our next adventure would be.

Epilogue

One year later

JARED CARRIED THE SUITCASE DOWN to the car and helped my very pregnant self into the front seat. He ran around to the other side, hopped in the driver's seat, and peeled away from the curb.

I put my hand on Jared's arm. "I'm fine. You don't have to rush. It will be hours yet."

"Did you call your parents?"

"Yes. They'll meet us at the hospital."

Once at the hospital, I was wheeled away to the maternity ward while Jared took care of the paperwork. I got settled in a room and smiled when I saw my mother walk through the door. "Mom, I'm so glad you're here."

"I wouldn't be anywhere else."

Another contraction wracked my body while my mother held my hand. "Breathe through it, honey. You can do it."

"Where's Jared?"

"He'll be here in a minute. Don't worry. He won't miss this."

It wasn't long before Jared joined me in the room.

The nurses checked my progress every hour. Labor was progressing, but slowly. After eight hours of labor the doctor came in and examined me. "Mrs. Castian, you're almost there—nine centimeters. We're going to take you to the delivery room now."

Jared had stepped out for a moment to update Steve and Danielle, and he wasn't back yet.

"No. Wait. I need my husband!"

"I'm right here, babe," Jared said, rushing to my side.

"Okay, let's go have a baby," the doctor said.

It didn't take long once we were in the delivery room for our child to be born—a beautiful healthy baby girl.

I looked at Jared, who had tears in his eyes. "Can you believe we made something so wondrous?" I asked as the doctor laid the baby on my chest. Before Jared had a chance to answer, I was wracked by another painful contraction. The nurse quickly took the baby from me.

The doctor felt my belly. "Time to push again," he said.

I opened my mouth to ask how our daughter was doing, when another contraction hit me.

Jared squeezed my hands. "Almost done, sweetheart."

"You're doing great. The head is crowning, almost finished," the doctor said.

"I'm so tired, I can't do it anymore," I wailed slumping back against the pillows.

Jared wiped the sweat from my face and put his arm around my shoulders. "I know you're tired, but it's almost over."

His quiet strength helped me push again and again. Within five minutes, our second child was born—a healthy boy.

Jared grabbed my hand and brought it to his lips. "My darling Ellie, you've given me two of the most perfect gifts a man could ask for."

Tears flowed down my cheeks. "Twins—can you believe it? We have twins."

Jared leaned over and kissed me with all the love and devotion he possessed. "I love you, Ellie. Don't worry about anything. We've got everything ready for these two little bundles and we'll figure things out, just like we always do."

As the nurse took my baby boy from my chest, I looked at my husband. He was pulling something out of his pocket and unwrapped the plastic bag. He held up a sprig of mistletoe.

"This is from the day you consented to be my wife—the happiest day of my life."

"You kept the mistletoe from our first Christmas?" I asked.

"Of course. Now hush while I kiss my extraordinary wife under the mistletoe."

Happy tears flowed down my cheeks. My life with Jared was everything I could have wished for, and with twin babies, I knew we were in for the adventure of our lives. "I love you, Jared Castian," I said before his lips met mine in a perfect kiss under the mistletoe.

THE END

Dear Reader,

Thank you for reading *Love and Kisses Christmas Collection.* I hope you enjoyed the stories and will consider leaving a review. Reviews are the best way for an author to know how a reader feels about the story and they are very much appreciated.

If you'd like to be informed about new releases, be sure to sign up for my newsletter at my blog, TWO ENDS OF THE PEN (https//:twoendsofthepen.blogspot.com).

Warm regards,

Debra

Debra Elizabeth

Other Titles by Debra Elizabeth

LOVING A BILLIONAIRE Series
An Accidental Wedding, Book 1

AGE OF INNOCENCE Regency Romance Series
Love by Secrets, Book 1
Love by Deception, Book 2
Dare to Love a Spy, Book 3

Love by Chance
CONTEMPORARY ROMANCE SHORT STORY

Love on the Beach
CONTEMPORARY ROMANCE NOVELLA

Second Chance Christmas
CONTEMPORARY ROMANCE SHORT STORY

NEW ENGLAND ROMANCE Series
CONTEMPORARY ROMANCES
Summer of Love, Book 1
Christmas Wedding Wishes, Book 2
Waiting for Love, Book 3
An Unexpected Love, Book 4
A Fairytale Romance, Book 5
Mistletoe Kisses, Book 6

About the Author

DEBRA ELIZABETH IS THE romance pen name for fantasy author Debra L. Martin. She has been writing stories since her teens and decided to finally publish her romance stories under a pen name so as not to confuse her fantasy fans. She publishes epic and urban fantasy with her co-author and brother, David W. Small. A full list of all of her books can be found at her blog, Two Ends of the Pen. She loves to hear from fans. You can contact her at dlmartin6@yahoo.com

Debra lives in New England with her husband and two kitties.

Made in the USA
Middletown, DE
06 August 2019